Copyright © 2020 Tim R

All rights reserve

The characters and events portrayed in this book are fictitious. Any similarity to real persons, living or dead, is coincidental and not intended by the author.

No part of this book may be reproduced, or stored in a retrieval system, or transmitted in any form or by any means, electronic, mechanical, photocopying, recording, or otherwise, without express written permission of the publisher.

ISBN-13: 978-1-952412-03-5

Cover design: Christopher Doll

Published By: Vagabond Publishing

Printed in the United States of America

Contents

One

Two

Three

Four

Five

Six

Seven

Eight

Nine

Ten

Eleven

Twelve

Thirteen

Fourteen

Fifteen

Sixteen

Seventeen

Eighteen

Nineteen

Twenty

Twenty One

Twenty Two

Twenty Three

Twenty Four

Twenty Five

Twenty Six

Twenty Seven

ONE

Natalia Avila flopped down on her bunk and groaned with exhaustion. She'd spent the last ten hours crawling through tight service tunnels, patching in new cables and conduits as the ship's systems were overhauled. The *Waterloo* was the oldest Coalition frigate still in service, and the powers that be on the planet below had finally decided to throw a few credits into bringing her up to snuff with the rest of the small fleet. Engineering and Technical teams had been combing the ship for weeks, and she fully expected to keep working long shifts for a few more months before all the replacement systems were fully online and the old stuff had been pulled out.

Debating whether to grab a shower before dropping into well-deserved sleep, Nat felt the hard plastic case of a tablet poking her in the back. Sore muscles protested as she reached underneath to pull the device out, and she tapped the screen to wake the display. *Might as well check my messages while I decide*, she thought as she flipped through icons and touched the one for her personal email. Amidst all of the usual advertisements and notifications of posts on her social media accounts, there were two messages received a few hours earlier and marked as urgent. One was from her parents on Earth, living in the mountains outside Mexico City. The other was from her sister who lived and worked in Aldrin dome on Luna.

Brow furrowed, she tried to remember the last time her family had sent anything that was marked for urgent delivery. Pressing the first message, she was surprised to see wild panic and fear in her mother's eyes. "Mija," the woman began, "please tell me it isn't true. Let us know that you're okay. Just call us!"

Nat stared at the screen for a minute, trying to figure out what her mother could be worried about. She opened the simple text from her sister to see if it explained things. *Nat, I know a lot of people are dismissing this, but I know Erik. He's not the kind of man who'd try to incite panic without reason. We need to take his warning seriously. Talk to your superiors, if you can, and make sure they don't mark it down as a message from another crazy kook.*

No more enlightened by the second message, she switched over to the news feeds. The screen was filled with red-bordered articles marked URGENT. She tapped to open the first one. Reading through the hastily written article, she learned about the message sent by a Guild freighter captain named Erik Frost and his warnings of some kind of Syndicate super ship. There was a link to his video message, and she pressed the button to play it. The man who appeared on the screen had brownish blonde hair that was cut short but sticking up in all directions. His vivid blue eyes were turned on the camera with a beseeching gaze, as his lips moved to speak the words that had sparked disdain with a scattering of panic.

"I am Erik Frost, captain of the Guild freighter *Vagabond.* My crew and I accepted a job several months ago to deliver cargo to a so-called black site." An image of a cargo container replaced his face on the screen, and Nat examined it as he continued to speak. She had seen a lot of shipments pass through the freighter, especially in recent months with the overhaul. Something about the look of this one gave her chills. It made her think of the crates of updated railgun systems that had arrived the week before.

The picture on the screen switched to a view of the Syndicate warship that the captain claimed had imprisoned them. It was hard to grasp how big or small the ship was with nothing in the picture to provide a frame of reference, but it certainly looked nothing like the frigates she was familiar with. There were a few lights across the black hull, but those could either be small running lights or an illuminated large docking bay. She returned her attention to the captain's words and her mouth dropped open.

"The Syndicate will use the heavy cruiser to destroy the Mars scientific outposts, and then the Coalition dome on Luna. Coalition cities on Earth will be targeted until that government folds."

Closing the newsfeed, she hurriedly opened a video call with her sister. "Come on, come on," she muttered as she waited for the call to be answered. It was only a few hours after midnight, but she couldn't imagine her sister being asleep after something like that message.

The call was finally answered. The woman in the video feed looked harried and completely drained. Dexterity Avila's eyes were drooping and washed out, and her skin looked almost gray. In the background, Nat could see men and women rushing around the offices of the Transport

Guild headquarters and hear multiple conversations being carried out in urgent tones.

"Nat, you got my message?"

"I just saw it, Dex. What in the hell is going on? Are you sure this is something we can take seriously?"

The camera shifted to show the view behind her sister, where an imposing man in an expensively cut suit was standing outside the door of an office barking orders at the people around him. "The Guild president believes it," Dex told her as the view shifted back to her tired face. "It'll be months before that Syndicate warship gets here from the belt, but he's already recalling all Guild freighters and telling us to make arrangements to get off Luna in case Aldrin really is a target."

Nat gasped and shook her head. Vaguely, she heard the door of the cabin hiss as someone entered. "Are you going to go home to mom and dad? When will you leave?"

"I'm not leaving until there's no choice," her sister told her resolutely. "There's too much to be done here. We need to make sure our crews are safe, reach out to our contacts in the mining colonies and on Deimos, and check in with our government liaisons. The Guild rep in the Syndicate capital is already trying to get a meeting with someone on the Executive Committee to get their response."

"If this is really happening, Dex, make sure you're off Luna before that ship arrives. Mom could never get over losing you."

"Nat, you're the one we're all worried about."

"Huh? Why worry about me? I'm not in a spot that your Captain Frost said was in danger."

Smiling wryly, Dex touched the screen. "You're on a Coalition frigate, manita. Who do you think they're going to send out to try and stop a warship when they realize it's on the way?"

"Oh." Nat was struck speechless. After three years in the Navy, serving on a ship that had never gone farther from Earth than short patrols to Mars, she'd come to think of it as little more than a typical workplace. Sure, the ship had railguns and torpedoes, but since they'd never been used aside from training exercises there were few on board who thought there could ever be real danger to the frigate. The stalemate between the Coalition and the Syndicate had dragged on for so long that their guards had been lowered and inertia had set in.

"I'll be fine," she finally said. "I need to call mom before she worries herself sick. Don't work yourself to death, Dex, and check in with me if you hear anything more."

"Same, Nat. I love you." The video screen went black as the call was ended. Nat closed her eyes and took a deep calming breath.

"That's a messed up situation, isn't it?" a voice asked.

She turned to see her bunkmate leaning against the bulkhead by the door. Janet Li worked a communications station on the bridge, and the two women shared the same shift. It made them perfectly fitted to share a cabin, since there was no threat of one waking the other while getting ready to go on shift or coming back.

"I can't believe no one in Engineering was talking about it. If I hadn't decided to check my messages before conking out, I still wouldn't know anything about it."

"You should have seen how it stirred up the command staff when that message came through in the middle of my shift. The lieutenant on duty called up the XO, who called in Captain Andrews. Before you know it there were half a dozen officers clustered around a video screen in the conference room. I heard the Fleet Admiral had every ship's command staff involved, along with the administrators of Aldrin and Deimos."

Nat sat up, flipping her legs around to hang down from the side of her bunk. "They're taking it seriously then?"

Janet shrugged, walking over to her locker to change out of her uniform. "No one's really sure. The meeting was still going on when my shift ended, but then it'd only started half an hour before." Flipping her long black hair over a shoulder, she turned to look at Nat. "That was your sister, right? The one who works for the Guild."

"Yeah, Dexterity. She knows that Erik Frost guy, and says he's trustworthy. Sounds like their leadership is definitely taking it seriously."

"Like she said, it'll be months before any ship can reach Earth from the belt. We'll know for sure what's going on long before that happens." Janet shrugged and disappeared into the small washroom with her bag of toiletries.

Nat spent several minutes with her thoughts racing. She finally shook them off as much as she could and called her mother to give a quick reassurance. After promising to visit the next time she got leave and could return planet side, she ended the call. She slipped out of the jumpsuit she wore as part of the engineering crew, and crawled into the zippered gel-filled sleeping bag that kept them safe in the event of any erratic maneuvers the ship had to perform. Relaxing into the warmth of the snug bed, she cycled through news reports for most of an hour until she was so tired she couldn't keep her eyes open any longer. Slipping the tablet into a pouch on the wall of the bunk, she shifted around to get comfortable and was asleep in moments.

Stopping in at the galley before starting her afternoon shift, Nat wasn't surprised to find everyone in the room was chatting about the message from the *Vagabond*. She could hear one ensign loudly proclaiming that the freighter captains were known to be scoundrels who would do anything for a credit, and he couldn't believe that anyone would take such a message seriously. Not far away, a handful of crew from various sections of the ship were huddled together, discussing the projected path of the warship and where their families should be sent to be safe from any attacks.

After dropping her empty tray into a recycling slot, she walked through the ship to reach Engineering on the lowest decks. People she passed in the corridor had worried expressions, and more than one looked as if they'd had no sleep at all since the previous day. There had been no ship-wide announcements yet, which worried her more than anything. If the Fleet Admiral and his staff had decided there was no reason to believe the warnings, then the captain would have announced it within hours of the message coming through. To wait this long told her they were either still in discussion with all the fleet officers or had decided to accept the warning as fact and were preparing to act on the information.

Walking into Engineering, she was waved over by one of the men who crawled through service corridors with her. “Did you hear?” he asked.

“Yeah, I saw the message last night after shift.”

“Not that,” he scoffed. “One of my friends on the team installing the last of the new railguns said two Syndicate frigates headed out in the direction of the belt this morning. He said their engines were burning hot and hard from what he could see.”

Nat raised her eyebrows. “I wonder what they’re doing. It’s supposed to be their ship out there, so why rush off after it?”

Shrugging, the crewman started searching for someone else to share his news with. “That video from the Frost guy said the ship was lightly crewed. Maybe those frigates are carrying more people out to fill the empty spots.” He hurried away from her as a new person entered from the corridor.

She had an uneasy feeling that his quick guess may prove to be more correct than he’d have expected. If she were in command of the Syndicate Navy, the first thing she’d do after the secret was out would be to get the cruiser everything needed to be a larger threat. Her jaw clenched as she thought about how this development put the *Waterloo* one step closer to being called into service to meet the new threat head on.

Once her shift started, the menial tasks that were on her schedule quickly took over her thoughts. Even when working to connect wiring to a new panel, something she'd done a hundred times before, she needed to put all her attention into the job to ensure it was done correctly. That need to focus only on the job and let any other worries melt away was one of the things that drew her to the Engineering department when she joined the Navy.

During her lunch break, she got comfortable in the tight confines of a service corridor that was only a few feet in height and width, and pulled a meal bar from her pocket. Munching on the grainy bar that had a taste reminiscent of apples and cinnamon, she thought of the Syndicate cruiser for the first time in hours. She grumbled to herself about the job that kept her so out of touch while on duty. The corridors that housed the frigate's wiring and electronics were heavily shielded to prevent any kind of disruption from errant signals, which also kept any tablet brought into the corridors disconnected from the ship's network. Nat had stopped toting her old tablet around during shift a few months into her posting on the *Waterloo*. Fighting a brief temptation to leave the service tunnel and check on any updates, she balled up the wrapper from her meal bar and shoved it into a pocket to dispose of later. She turned back to her work and was soon lost in the minutiae of rewiring panels for several more hours.

Crawling out of the small service tunnel at the end of her shift, Nat took a minute to stretch out her muscles and enjoy the freedom of having enough room to extend her arms and legs. The lieutenant in charge of her shift, Mags Richtaus, sauntered over to check in and verify which tasks had been successfully completed. They spent a few minutes running down the list, and discussing some items that would need to be added or require extra work.

"I know you guys are out of touch in the tunnels," Mags said at the end. "Captain is making a ship-wide announcement in about ten minutes. He wants to catch everyone between shifts."

"Thanks, lieutenant. Is it about the *Vagabond* message?"

"I'd say the odds are overwhelmingly in favor of that. Get cleaned up while you can."

Nat gratefully headed for her cabin, situated near midship since she and her bunkmate worked at opposite ends of the frigate. She made it through the door before the announcement started, and found Janet laying in the top bunk having just returned from her own shift. "Do you know what the captain's going to say?" she asked, stripping out of the dusty and greasy jumpsuit.

"Not a clue," Janet replied, shaking her head as she kept her eyes on her tablet. "I don't think it's going to be good, though, based on how much frowning my lieutenant was doing near the end of shift."

"You heard about the Syndicate frigates heading out toward the belt this morning?"

"This morning? Nat, they've been leaving Earth orbit all day. Six at the last count, with the last one departing two hours ago."

Nat turned sharply. "That's their whole fleet, isn't it?"

"Two more left," Janet corrected. "One is in orbit on the far side of the planet, over the Syndicate capital in Hong Kong. The other was last seen farther in system, doing scientific exploration around Venus."

"Still, that's a lot of firepower heading for the outer system, leaving the Syndicate leadership exposed. If our prime minister or the Admiralty ordered it, we could take out their one frigate here and start landing Marines on their cities."

"Until that giant cruiser arrived with six frigates escorting it. Then we'd lose everything we gained and more."

"What are we going to do to fight against that ship, anyway?" Nat asked quietly, entering the washroom for a quick shower. The small stall had several dozen nozzles placed to spritz water onto the skin from all angles at once, to allow for minimal water usage. Water sprayed for five seconds, the bather soaped up, water sprayed out again for ten seconds to wash the soap off, and the process was complete. Exiting back into the cabin rubbing a towel over her short black curls, Nat was just in time to hear the tones sounding throughout the ship to alert listeners to a ship-wide announcement.

"Crew of the *Waterloo*, this is Captain Andrews." She straightened up unconsciously at the deep tones of the captain's voice, three years of ingrained discipline taking over. "By now, all of you have seen the video sent out by the freighter captain, and his claims about the cruiser named *Indomitable*. The command staff and I have been in conference with the Admiralty and our other frigates for the last twenty-four hours. In light of the actions of the Syndicate frigates, and with confirmation received from the sensors of the colony on Interamnia, Fleet Admiral Holgerson has decided to take these warnings seriously.

"Effective immediately, the Coalition government has suspended leave. All personnel have been recalled to their ships. Our refit will continue, but at an increased pace. Additional crew and technicians will be sent over from the orbital station to assist. All frigates will be placed in orbit around Earth until the Admiralty and prime minister have a chance to confer and decide upon an appropriate course of action.

"In the coming days, the officers of your departments will meet with you to pass on any new orders or to rearrange the priority of work. Our primary goal at this moment is to complete the refit and modernization of the *Waterloo* within two weeks so we're ready to participate in any action that is required of us. I know there are few aboard who have been in battle before, but I won't hesitate to say that the prospect looms large for us at this moment. Thank you all for your continued hard work."

A trilling tone indicated the announcement was at an end. Nat realized that she was still holding the towel to her hair and had not moved during the speech. Tossing the towel into the sanitizer, she crawled into her bunk and zipped herself in. "What do you think?" she asked, staring up at the bottom of the bunk over her head.

"I think I joined the Navy a few years too late," Janet replied. "Two more years, and I could have taken my ten year service benefits and found a cushy job on the planet to keep me comfortable."

"This is going to change everything, isn't it?" Nat asked quietly, trying to imagine being on a ship that was attacking and being attacked by another.

"I just hope we're both around to see what it changes everything to," Janet said morosely. She flipped the switch that sent the room into darkness lit only by the light of the woman's tablet as she kept reading news stories.

Two

"I'm getting messages routing through Luna," Mira said, tapping urgently at the screen in front of her. "Sending them over to your display, cap."

"Thanks," Erik said, setting aside the cooling cup of coffee he was trying to enjoy during the respite between short acceleration burns as the *Vagabond* tried to catch up to the Syndicate cruiser. It had been less than a week since the *Indomitable* attack on Interamnia, destroying the colony and killing everyone there. He was resolute in his desire to help fight against the warship in whatever way he could. Right now, that meant trying to reach Luna and Earth as quickly as possible.

The first few messages he perused quickly and filed away. More government officials trying to apologize for not believing his warnings without really apologizing, using words that almost made it sound like his fault for not sending a warning sooner to prevent the disastrous loss of hundreds of lives on the mining colony. He found a message from Dex in the list, and pressed the screen to open it on the holo display hovering two feet in front of him where only he could see the screen.

"Erik, I'm so sorry about the Murphys. I can't believe the Syndicate would do something as heinous as blowing up an entire colony." Her eyes were red from exhaustion, but he could see deep sympathy in them as she looked into the camera. "President Meyers wanted me to express his condolences, as well. He was trying to get answers from the Syndicate's Executive Committee, but they expelled our representative last night. I hear they also told the Coalition ambassador and his staff to leave their territories within forty-eight hours or face the consequences. Things are not going well here." She closed her eyes, and he could see the frustration and fear combating in her expression.

"The last two Syndicate frigates remain in orbit over Earth. The scientific mission around Venus was cancelled and that ship arrived yesterday afternoon. I've been in contact with a few people I know in the Coalition Admiralty, but no one can say what might have been loaded onto the other six frigates before they left to rendezvous with the *Indomitable.* President Meyers agrees with the majority consensus that personnel and weapons are the most likely things being transported. So be careful out there, Erik. Don't go rushing into anything without checking it out first. You still owe me that drink, remember." Dex smiled, making him blush.

"Oh, before I forget, I got the message with those research notes from the guy you knew on Interamnia, Robert Silva. I checked in with Meyers and he sent it out to a few folks he knows on Earth and Mars. We both think it looks like promising research, but I'm not sure what kind of resources can be put into it until the current threats are past. Send me updates, okay? Reassure me that old junk heap you call home hasn't fallen apart around you." With a sad smile, she looked into the camera for a few moments and then reached out to end the recording.

Sighing deeply, Erik leaned back in his command chair and went through the rest of the messages. There was nothing else worth his attention. He slammed a fist on his armrest in frustration.

"Everything okay over there, cap?"

"Yeah, Mira, it's fine. I just can't believe the Coalition hasn't done anything even after they learned about the destruction of Interamnia. What kind of atrocity is going to have to happen to make them take notice?"

The chair of the pilot's station creaked as it was turned to face him, the svelte brunette looking at him with a ghost of a smile. "It's only been a few days for them, cap. Governments move slowly, and they can't just decide to send their ships out on the attack right away. Give them some time to process what's been happening."

"Time," he spat out. "If they keep taking their time to do everything, the *Indomitable* is going to be in orbit over the planet with debris from destroyed frigates raining down before they make a decision."

"I know you're angry, but don't let emotion override your logic. We all feel the loss of the colony, even those of us who didn't know John and Sally. And we all have someone on Luna or Earth that we're afraid for. It's worse for me, Jen and Tom since we haven't even had a chance to tell our friends and family that we didn't die seven years ago on the *Telemachus*. Can you imagine how hard it would be to hear that my dad died not knowing I was still here and on the way to help save him? Our messages to Earth are getting blocked, even when we try to route through Luna."

Erik rubbed his face, as if wiping away his anger. "You're right, Mira. I'm getting too wrapped up in my own frustration. I'm sorry for not thinking about what the rest of you might be going through." His eyes flickered over to the terminal that displayed the internal feeds from the cargo bay, where the rest of the crew was working to cut through the locks on the Syndicate container. "After the next acceleration burn, let's take a longer break and gather in the galley. I think we should all have a chance to vent our feelings to each other."

Mira nodded once, smiling widely as she turned back to her station. Erik sent a short message to the crew telling them about the proposed meeting, and then left the control room to take his coffee cup back into the galley to dump it in the sanitizer. He realized with a start that he had been standing in the same spot for several minutes, staring at nothing and lost in thought. When he wasn't remembering time spent on board with the Murphys, he was thinking of Tuya and how she'd run deeper into the cruiser on a mission to save a brother she had thought dead for seven years, while the rest of them had to rush in the opposite direction to escape and send warnings out to the system. A large part of him wished he could have blindly followed after her, dreaming of wrapping his hands around the throat of the admiral in charge of the Syndicate warship. He didn't even know who the admiral was, but he knew that he wanted that person as dead as his friends were.

He relaxed his jaw and his hands, telling himself to calm down as he returned to his command chair. The countdown to the next acceleration burn was rapidly draining, and he flipped on the ship's intercom system to tell the others to return to their crash couches to prepare for the crushing six G forces they would be under for fifteen minutes.

It had startled him several days into their desperate race to reach the mining colony to realize that he hadn't even noticed the ship's rattles and shaking as more than a background nuisance. He even stopped worrying about the ship falling apart around him as they pushed the *Vagabond* to her limits. Sitting in his command chair during the latest acceleration burn, sinking into the soft gel until only a small part of his body was not covered by it, he wondered if his concerns had always been nothing more than something to occupy his mind during the long voyages between ports.

As soon as the burn was complete, he returned to his cabin to pull off stale clothes and take a quick shower before pulling on a clean jumpsuit. It pained him to admit it, but he felt better than he had in five days once he was clean. It was as if the water and air jets had washed away most of his anger and grief along with the dirt. He realized that he'd been neglecting the mental health of himself and the crew for too long.

Entering the galley, he found that Jen was the only other person there. He smiled as he noted that she too had showered and changed before the gathering. Filling a cup with instant coffee, really just heated water that ran through a small bit of dried coffee grounds, he motioned with his cup to ask if she wanted one.

"No thanks," she said gruffly.

Erik straddled a bench across the table from her, and sipped at the watery brown drink. He and Jen had gotten off to a bad start, with him tackling her as she broke into the cabin he and his crew had been imprisoned in on the Syndicate warship. They had wrestled on the ground for a short while before Altan Sansar had introduced his group as the survivors of the *Telemachus*, and he hadn't had the chance to apologize to her in between all of the action and danger since.

"I'm sorry for the way we met," he said hesitantly. "You know, tackling you to the ground and all that."

Jen glared at him for a moment, but then looked away. "Don't worry about it, captain. I would have attacked you in the same way if our roles had been reversed. I'm not holding a grudge or anything."

"You sure? It seems like you've been mad at me ever since."

She shook her head, and met his eyes. "I'm mad at myself. I had two older brothers who bullied me mercilessly when I was growing up, and it just brought all those bad memories flooding back when you had me wrapped up so easily."

Erik reached across to place a hand over hers. "Jen, I'm so sorry. I hate that I had to remind you of something like that."

She shrugged and pulled her hand away as Isaac entered. "It's not your fault. Just something I haven't taken the time to deal with since that night."

"That's the reason I wanted to get us all together," he told her. "I think we all have a lot of stuff to work through. We can do that better if we talk it out together."

Isaac joined them at the table, sitting very close to Jen and offering her a shy smile that was returned with true affection. Erik hid a smile behind his coffee cup as he turned to see Fynn walk into the galley with Tom. The two men were chatting about an issue they were working on in the engine room. Mira followed half a minute behind, and the small galley was filled with the buzz of conversation as everyone grabbed food or drink and got settled at the long table.

"Okay," Erik said, grabbing their attention. "I wanted to get everyone together so we can discuss everything that's happened lately. We've all lost friends, and we've experienced the loss of hundreds more people. I know it's been affecting me, and I'm sure you all feel it, too." He glanced around to see a few nods from the others.

"Losing the Murphys and leaving Tuya behind on *Indomitable* has been fueling my anger and rage, driving me to chase after the cruiser with everything we have. If it wasn't for Mira calling me out earlier, I would probably still be pushing the ship and all of you harder than I have any right to." He rubbed a hand over his face and leaned his elbows on the table, worn smooth from decades of use.

"None of us blame you for that, Erik." Fynn tapped the table as he spoke. "Sally was stuck on that asteroid when the damned AI started her power trip, and I know John would've always wanted to have been there with her at the end if he had decided to stay on the *Vagabond* instead of leaving to be with her."

"Yeah," Isaac agreed softly. "Those two were more in love than anyone I've ever seen. It would have been absolute hell for them if one had survived without the other." The tech unconsciously reached out a hand to wrap his fingers in Jen's as he spoke.

Jen cleared her throat. "I didn't know the Murphys, but I did get to know Tuya a little bit as we were escaping from the Syndicate cruiser. She struck me as a very strong willed woman, the kind who did what she thought needed doing no matter what your opinion might have been. A lot like Altan, actually." She smiled at the memories of her old crewmate. "I have no doubt those two are still on that ship causing all kinds of trouble, and neither of them would blame you or us for escaping without them."

"Maybe so," Erik said. He paused, trying to think of a way to put his feelings into words. "I just can't stop thinking I could have done more. You know? Like there was something I should have thought about that could have stopped that cruiser then." Shrugging, he looked around at the others. "It's hard to express it all. Anyone else want to talk about what's weighing on their minds?"

THREE

Huddled inside one of the small storage closets in a part of the ship that saw little traffic, Tuya Sansar ripped open a high protein meal bar she'd swiped from a storage room and took a large bite. In the confusion of the *Vagabond*'s escape she'd been able to kill or injure half a dozen Marines after parting from the group. She'd been careful to avoid Marines after a time, so they would believe she had left on the freighter with the rest of the *Vagabond* crew. The last of the Marines she confronted had been glad to give her directions to the holding cells where her brother was being kept. She'd been forced to kill the Marine to keep her goal secret.

It hadn't taken long for her to realize that she couldn't rush in immediately and rip the cell door open to have a happy reunion with Altan. Instead, she had to infiltrate the ship. For the last couple of weeks, she had crept through silent corridors and ducked into empty rooms whenever she could hear one of the crew or diminished Marine patrols approaching. She ate when she could find food, carried a small bottle of water on her belt that she refilled when possible, and melted into the shadows.

If the ship had carried more than a small scattering of crew and Marines, her task would have been markedly more difficult. As it was, she was able to move through the ship with relative ease most of the time. She found herself hiding in closets and service tunnels for only an hour or two before the area was clear again. The temptation to take out lone crew members wandering the halls had been strong, but so far she'd resisted so as to remain undetected.

The acceleration burns had been rough, especially the first burn from where the cruiser had been hiding. She'd found a vacant cabin with a crash couch that she could use when she had warning of a burn approaching, but had been caught out a few times and blacked out once from the stress on her body. If not for her cybernetic implants, she felt sure she wouldn't have survived those periods of high gravity. The ship had been holding a steady thrust of a quarter G for more than a week, allowing her to get around the ship more easily.

Now, she was resting in a dusty storage closet only a few hundred meters from the holding cells where Altan was being kept. At least she hoped he was still being kept there, and had not been moved or executed. The thought of losing her brother for a second time was enough to make her fists clench and start a low growl deep in her throat. Her plan was to approach the holding cells in the early morning hours and try to get a view into the rooms to discover if Altan was there and how many Marines were guarding him.

Tossing the protein bar wrapper into a corner, she looked over the armor pieces she had salvaged from opponents she had faced during the escape. Tuya knew the missing armor would be assumed to have been taken along on the *Vagabond*, so she had been careful to remove the built in tablets in the forearm pieces to disable any tracking software. She cleaned blood from a few spots on the shiny armor, and adjusted straps so the pieces would fit snugly to her small frame. With great luck, one of the Marines taken down in the fights had been a female about her size, and she'd recovered the chest armor that fit her much better than any of the pieces pulled from the male soldiers.

When the clock in her head indicated that it was near the end of the overnight shift, Tuya strapped the armor on over the black skintight biosuit she had stolen from a sanitizing drawer in the early days. Fully outfitted, she looked just like one of the Syndicate soldiers and could blend in as long as someone passing in the corridors didn't try to engage her in conversation. She kept her wrists turned in and close to her body to hide the missing displays.

Stepping out of the storage closet, she checked the corridor to ensure she was alone and then turned in the direction of the holding cells. She kept a steady pace as she walked, holding her head high like a typical Marine would, crisply saluting any officers she passed while ignoring the non-rates and regular crew. The stun pistol she carried was holstered at her side, the strap loosened so she could draw quickly if needed. It pained her to leave behind the flechette rifle taken during the escape, but the lethal rounds were tightly controlled and it had proven impossible to refill her empty magazines.

As she approached the holding cells, Tuya was greeted with the sight of a guard post manned by a single Marine standing at attention. The doors lining the small corridor behind him were smooth and sturdy, with small displays that could be turned on to show the room inside. Another Marine was sitting at the rear of the corridor, shielded by the high wall of a small desk that exposed only his head and provided an excellent firing position to defend the hallway from attackers.

There was no indicator to tell her which of the cells were occupied, if any. She had no doubt that the controls for the doors were on the desk at the far end of the corridor. Tuya could see the black lenses of cameras in the corners above the desk that told her the hallway was being watched from another security desk elsewhere on the cruiser. Grunting in disgust, she continued past with only a brief greeting to the Marine on guard. She made several turns to check her rear and be sure there was no one following before she returned to the storage closet that had been her home for the last few days.

Stripping off the armor pieces and dropping them to the floor in frustration, Tuya snarled and slammed a fist against the wall. It left a faint dent. Rescuing her brother from the holding cells was looking more difficult than ever. She knew she'd have to find another way rather than the direct assault she had planned. She leaned back against the cool bulkhead and slid down to sit with arms wrapped around her knees.

Tuya had felt the railguns firing several days after parting from her crew and the survivors of the *Telemachus*. Overheard conversation had reassured her that the freighter managed to get away, but when she felt the shudder of the heavy weapons firing later on it had sparked fears that the chase was over and her friends had been blown into atoms. She'd tried to get more information, but the displays on the ship were locked down and only worked after an ocular scan to verify which systems a person had access to. Leaving behind a cracked screen, she hadn't tried another and was left hoping that her friends still lived.

Running away from Erik and the others had been a difficult decision. At the same time, she had known there was no way she could leave her brother behind on the Syndicate warship after finding out he was still alive. In the emotions of the moment, it had seemed a simple thing to rush through the ship to rip open the cell door and be able to see and touch Altan again.

In the ensuing weeks, she'd found herself missing the presence of her captain and crewmates, a family that she'd never expected to have when she started traveling the stars. There had been times she found herself wanting to talk things out with Frost, to get his opinions on what she was doing and see if there was a better way.

Her eyes drooped as she indulged in the memories of her old life aboard the *Vagabond.* A small part of her still held out hope that she would one day be part of the crew again, but a larger part knew that she was more likely to die on the Syndicate cruiser trying to rescue her brother. It was a price she was willing to pay for the chance to see him once more.

FOUR

Wiping sweat-soaked strands of hair from her face, Nat resolved for the thousandth time to grow her hair out long enough to be tied back while working. She knew it wouldn't be bothering her so much if she'd had time over the last three weeks to get her curly locks cut, but the frenzied pace of the upgrades and retrofitting had left her with little time outside of work. She returned to her cabin each night so exhausted that she fell into sleep without even stripping off the dirty jumpsuit. The next morning she woke feeling just as tired and had time to change and grab a quick meal before crawling into the next section of service tunnels to continue rewiring and replacing.

There were mutters of discontent from her fellow engineering crew in the last few days, complaints that even with the extra hands sent over from the orbital station they were being overworked and pushed too hard to meet a deadline that was impossible to hit. She shared the sentiment, but also felt a pride in her ability to do the work. Nat felt confident that if they fell short it wouldn't be because her contribution wasn't up to snuff. Spending fourteen and fifteen hours a day crawling through the tight tunnels was taking a toll on her body, but she refused to let up until the work was complete.

They had received little new information since the captain's announcement to the ship. The rest of the Coalition's fleet of frigates had arrived to join the *Waterloo* in orbit, the last of them arriving only a few days before from a patrol around Mars. Always eager to keep pace with their rivals, the Coalition had eight frigates in operation. Along with the *Waterloo*, another was also in the process of modernization after more than two decades of service. Even the newest of the frigates had almost a decade of continuous service and was inferior to the more modern Syndicate ships.

The few times they'd been in the cabin at the same time over the last several weeks, Janet had shared news that the naval academy was graduating the latest class of cadets early to get them loaded into frigates to pad the crews. There was also talk of adding fighters to the frigates, shoving two or three into each ship's tightly packed cargo bays. Nat was too exhausted to debate the wisdom of such moves, but couldn't help feeling it was not enough to counter the overwhelming force of the Syndicate cruiser even if it was only partially equipped.

Nat traded messages with her mother and sister a few times over the weeks, letting them know that she was okay. She kept trying to talk Dex into leaving the Guild office on Aldrin dome before the threat of the cruiser was too close. Her sister always told her there was too much work yet to be done, and talked about some kind of scientific work she was coordinating with labs on Deimos and in Munich. Conversely, both her mother and sister kept trying to talk Nat into requesting a transfer to a safer posting on Earth or the Coalition orbital station, even after she explained that any such transfer would be denied.

On the planet below, she knew there was rioting and growing dissent as factions within the two superpowers fought to push for reconciliation before it was too late.

Some groups even denied the existence of the heavy cruiser, or claimed that the destruction of Interamnia was a propaganda event that had never happened. Nat had even heard the opinion expressed in the galley one morning, by a pampered ensign who'd been posted to the ship when it was a plum assignment seen as a stepping stone to a political career enhanced by a shining record of military service. Now that the threat of real war loomed, the woman had been speaking with trembling fear in her voice and sounded as if she were trying to reassure herself more than convince others.

Nat twisted the last pair of wires together, sliding them into the back of a new panel and clamping them in place to ensure a tight connection. A glance at her diagnostic kit showed that it was several hours past the end of her normal shift, and she groaned as she lay back in the sweltering tunnel to try and relax a cramp that had formed in her shoulders from holding her head at an awkward angle for so many weeks. The list of work for the day was finally complete, and she could crawl to the nearest service hatch to exit into the cooler, fresher air of a main corridor. With twice the number of people crawling through the tunnels, the increased body heat had overwhelmed the tight spaces.

She stumbled through the corridor as she returned to Engineering to drop off her tools and diagnostic kit. Half-hearted waves were shared with others ending or beginning shifts as she wordlessly left to return to her cabin where she would try to get enough sleep to feel a bit more rested the next morning. For the first week, she'd suffered nightmares of being caught in the service tunnels during an attack, but after that the exhaustion had overwhelmed her so much that she either no longer dreamed or could never remember them upon waking.

The door of the cabin swished open as she waved her hand in front of the sensor, and she kicked her boots off to lay wherever they landed. Janet was also working long shifts on the bridge, often pulling double duty to cover for people temporarily shifted to help out in other areas. Their shared space had grown more cluttered after several weeks of not having time to organize or clean. She flopped into her bunk, zipping it closed around her automatically. Her breathing slowed and she could feel her mind drifting into formless sleep when the cabin door opened and yelling from the corridor startled her awake.

Nat opened her eyes to see Janet standing in the open doorway, turned away to look down the corridor. "Whass goin on?" she slurred sleepily.

"Someone just set off a bomb in New York City. Right down the street from the Western Sector government buildings."

"What? Who did it?" Nat hurriedly unzipped and got out of her bunk, all thoughts of sleep blown from her mind as she rushed over to look out into the corridor.

"Let's go down to the rec room," Janet said. "They'll know more there."

The women joined a throng of other off-duty crew on the way to the recreational area, a room large enough to hold a gym, tables set up for gaming or meeting with groups to chat, and a lounge area with screens always displaying various entertainment programs. At the moment, all three of the screens were tuned to different news reports from the planet below.

Reporters stood in front of scenes of destruction, sirens wailing behind them. Rubble covered city streets, and medical personnel moved quickly through the background to get where they were most needed. An assault shuttle arrived behind one reporter, the air jets slowing its descent and sending lighter debris flying. Two squads of heavily armed soldiers disembarked, and split off to form barricades that would keep civilians away from the disaster zone.

"Our latest information is that over seven thousand dead and another fifteen thousand wounded," the reporter on the closest screen was saying. "An incendiary device was set off in the middle of the morning commute. There were large numbers of people on the sidewalks and streets at the time. Many more people were working in the buildings nearby most damaged in the blast. The Coalition governor for the Western Sector was in the building at the time of the explosion, but we're told he was immediately evacuated to a secure location far from the city shortly after."

"Dios mio," Nat whispered, holding a hand over her mouth as she watched the report. Janet had sunk down into a nearby chair, her face going pale. Nat turned to her. "Are you okay?"

"My parents live in New York," she said, looking at the tablet clenched tightly in one hand. "Only a few blocks from the government buildings. I sent them a message as soon as I heard the news, but I haven't gotten a response yet."

Kneeling down, Nat grabbed her hand and held it tightly. "The communications systems will be overloaded. I'm sure they're fine. They'll contact you when they can."

They held each other as they continued to watch the news reports, mostly rehashing the details of the attack and casualties over and over. There was speculation from the pundits and experts that the attack had to be an escalation by the Syndicate, a kind of government-sponsored terrorism. No proof had yet been found and no one had claimed credit. After a few hours, Nat felt her exhaustion once again and was barely able to keep her eyes open. She crawled into one of the comfortable cushioned chairs and curled up to fall asleep with the words of the reporters and her fellow crew members flowing over her.

"Nat." Someone was calling her name and shaking her gently. She reached out an arm to push them away so she could go back to sleep, but the shaking got more insistent. "Nat, you're going to miss your shift if you don't get moving."

Opening eyes that felt gummy, she saw Janet standing over her. The woman's face was still pale and the bags under her eyes were greatly exaggerated as a result.

"You look almost as tired as I feel," Nat said.

"I've been afraid to go to sleep, thinking I might miss my parents calling me." Janet rubbed a tear from her eye, and turned away. "I still can't get them, and they won't release a casualty list from the attack until the investigation is complete."

"I'm sorry, Janet. I should have stayed up with you." Nat rubbed at her eyes, jaws cracking as she yawned widely. "Have there been any updates on who attacked us?"

"Nothing but more speculation. The prime minister is supposed to give a speech in a few hours, so maybe we'll learn something then."

"Well, you'll learn something. I'll be stuck in yet another service tunnel with no access to the ship's network."

"Take breaks!" Janet told her firmly. "You never do, but you're allowed to take time to recharge so you can tackle your work with a clearer mind. Crawl out and check in when you're able."

Nat sighed. "You're right, if today isn't the day for that then I don't know when it will be. Let me know if you manage to get in touch with your parents."

Leaving Janet to return her attention to the rotating reporters and news desk anchors, Nat trailed through the corridors stopping to grab her tablet from their cabin before heading to the galley for a coffee to drink on the way to Engineering. She found the room buzzing with small groups of people talking about the latest attack, but avoided them to grab her tools and diagnostic kit and check her work schedule.

She stopped outside the first service hatch to power up her tablet. There were messages from her parents asking if she knew anything that wasn't on the news, but a conspicuous silence from her sister. She sent off a quick reply to her parents that she knew nothing more than what was shown on the networks, and then a message to her sister asking if everything was okay on Luna. Impatience kept her waiting, staring at the tablet screen until a reply came back that Dex was okay, just very busy with her work. Targeted by the same threatened attack on Aldrin dome, the Transport Guild had thrown in with the Coalition and dedicated their ships to transporting goods and fleet personnel wherever they were needed.

Slipping the tablet into a wide pocket on her thigh, Nat pulled the service hatch open and crawled through to begin another long shift of tight workspaces and finicky wiring.

Five

Lieutenant Roger Davis stood at attention in front of the narrow desk, his eyes locked on the bare wall above the superior officer's head. His hands were rigid at his side, and his mind wandered as the tirade he had tuned out of minutes earlier continued. It had been almost a month since the *Vagabond* and her crew made their daring escape from the Syndicate cruiser, and he still felt conflicted about the situation. As a long serving officer of the Syndicate Navy, and especially as a member of an elite squad trusted with the highest priority jobs, he knew he should feel bitter disappointment that the freighter crew had managed to kill or wound more than a dozen Marines in the process of making their escape. He *did* feel a large amount of disgust that the old *Telemachus* crew managed to assist and join the escape, and a larger amount for the Marine captain who was warned of the plan by one of that crew and then managed to botch the operation to capture both crews.

On the other hand, he'd spent most of a week aboard the *Vagabond* and gotten to know Erik Frost and his crew to a certain extent. He had liked all of them, even the cargo specialist he'd been required to take into custody and question after the ship was locked down to prevent the crucial cargo pod from being offloaded. It had pained him to have to be part of that interrogation, but he had taken personal responsibility for the four crew members to guarantee they would not be executed right away. He had sympathized with their desire to be free, and knew how much it hurt them to face the loss of their ship. But he also knew how important it had been to keep the secrecy of their ship and mission intact.

Which led to his being called to this office almost every day since the escape to be berated.

"...tried to tell the Admiral that he was making a mistake putting so much faith in you, Davis, but that man has a soft spot a mile wide where you're concerned. If it were up to me, I'd have you stripped of all rank and tossed into a cell right beside that Sansar fellow! Give me one more reason to do it, and I won't even stop to ask the admiral for his opinion."

Commander Guildersen finally trailed off as the quarter-hour rant came to a close. The heavyset older man looked as if the experience hurt him more than the recipient of his vitriol, with his round face scarlet and sweat dripping down from his sparse hairline. The collar of his uniform was tight around his neck at the best of times, but after the exertion of yelling at Davis it seemed to be cutting into his skin.

"Yes, Commander," Davis replied, glad that the session was nearing an end.

Guildersen stared at him for half a minute, breathing heavily and getting his temper under control. "The admiral and I are in agreement on one thing, Lieutenant. Now that the system knows of the *Indomitable*, your team is going to be called into action much sooner than expected. Our frigates are on the way with more personnel and supplies, and we should rendezvous with the first of them in three or four weeks. That will be an excellent time to test your skills, yes?"

Davis waited a moment to be sure that his input was really requested. "Yes, Commander. My team is ready and I welcome the opportunity to show their skills."

"Yes, well, we shall see what happens when the time comes. You'll have clearance for two training sessions on the hull each of the next three weeks, four hours per session with no one else outside the ship, as you requested. Make them count, lieutenant, because I assure you that no one but me will be happy if you fail." With a wolfish smile, the commander waved a dismissal.

Snapping a salute, Davis turned and exited the cabin. He relaxed his stance as soon as the doors closed behind him, and turned to walk to his team's training area. With a low chuckle, he remembered how he had presented himself as a computer specialist to the crew of the *Vagabond.* But then the smile faded from his face as he remembered the insertion pod that was still aboard the freighter when they escaped. The pods were extremely expensive hardware, only manufactured in one small factory deep in Syndicate territory on Earth, and as a result there had been one for each member of his team aboard the *Indomitable*. Now they were a pod short, and he would have to make the decision of who to leave out if a mission required using them.

Entering one of the vast cargo bays that had been set aside for his use, he found the other nine members of his elite assault and insertion team suited up and waiting. The armor they used was matte black, a single-piece suit that had light armor plating sewn into the ballistic fabric along with tubing to pump water that kept the wearer hot or cool depending on the mission parameters. Each assault suit had a suite of electronics onboard that controlled a heads-up display inside the full helmet along with a communications and sensor system that allowed the members of the team to detect threats and talk with each other on a band unused by any other devices.

"Sir, squad is present and ready for training," his sergeant reported, stepping forward to tap a fist over his heart in an informal salute.

"Excellent, start the exercise and I will monitor from control." Davis turned to enter a small room set up with displays filling one wall so that he could watch the training area from all directions. The cargo bay had been set up with false corridors and hull plating to mimic the breaching of a ship while facing resistance to reach a target. Another part of the bay was configured with city streets and a few building facades, with several floors set up inside that could become office or residential targets.

Settling into the high-backed chair, Davis switched the displays to show the exterior of the ship setting. He knew the two remaining squads of Marine soldiers onboard were filling the corridors within to provide a realistic resistance to a boarding operation. Their commanders were in charge of the deployment, and he resisted the urge to take a look at how they were set up. He liked to follow his team's action as if he were along with them, and judge their responses based on what he would do in the same situation without any knowledge of what waited around the next corner.

His sergeant and the eight soldiers dropped from the highest catwalk around the top of the cargo bay, strapped to lines that slowed their descent to mimic the speed and feel of using thrusters to travel through the vacuum of space. Using a rapid series of hand signals, Sergeant Anders split the team and they landed a few hundred meters apart, engaging magnetic locks in their boots.

While one member of each foursome pulled out a hand torch to cut through the plating, the other three kept a vigilant watch over the hull around them in case their approach had been detected. Within minutes, there was an opening in the plating large enough for each of the team to drop through and the expended torches were discarded. The first group to complete the cutting procedure waited a few seconds for the other to finish, and then the first member of each group dropped through the hole to land in the corridor below.

Davis threw up the display from each group leader's helmet camera onto the largest displays in front of him, watching their progress as the other assault troops dropped into the ship. Sergeant Anders dropped to join Group Two, knowing that Davis himself would be joining Group One in a real insertion. Once the corridors were secured, the two groups moved deeper into the ship. The target of today's training exercise was a computer core that ostensibly held intelligence and logistical data for the enemy forces.

Group One went toward the bow of the ship, two members darting forward as the other two covered with weapons facing either direction along the corridor. They bypassed the lift, earning an approving smile from Davis, and carefully entered the stairway to go down two decks. The team's briefing had provided information that the core was being kept in a secure room on that level.

Exiting the stairwell they met the first resistance, a squad of eight Marines set up behind a barricade down the hallway. Soft-headed flechette rounds filled the corridor, specially designed to cause no more than a bruise if they hit unprotected skin. The assault suit computers registered any hit and displayed the severity of a lethal round on the soldier's HUD and in the control center. The group leader sprinted across the corridor to crouch behind a bulkhead protrusion, while his three teammates leaned out from the stairwell to return fire on the Marine squad.

Group Two started aft from where they entered the ship, Anders placed in the middle of the formation and using the more powerful sensor suite in his assault armor to probe the corridors ahead. They encountered half-hearted resistance from a pair of Marines patrolling the corridor, but their overwhelming firepower soon had both Marines out of action and "dead" behind them.

When they found a service hatch that had a ladder connecting the decks of the ship, one of the assault soldiers popped the lock on the hatch and set it aside quietly. Waving the group through, Sergeant Anders kept a rearguard and watched the display from the first soldier down the ladder. The camera showed him and Davis a first-person view as the soldier carefully disengaged the lock on the hatch below and then pulled it into the service tunnel. The soldier then extracted a small camera on a long stalk, which he slowly slid out into the corridor to get a view of what was there. Anders and Davis saw the feed on a small box on their displays, showing an empty corridor.

The assault soldiers crawled through the hatch to form up in the corridor and provide cover until all five had exited and the hatch cover had been replaced on both ends of the ladder. They could hear the faint sounds of battle ahead, and Anders keyed his comms to check in on the other half of the team.

"Group One leader, Anders. Status."

"Sarge, taking heavy fire. Marine squad behind barricades. Estimate we are fifty meters from target location with enemy forces twenty meters aft of us."

"Maintain cover and return fire. I'll lead Two in from the rear and eliminate resistance." Static-filled squawks ended the communication, and Anders turned to signal to his group. With one soldier keeping an eye behind, they moved quickly and silently through the corridor as the sound of weapon fire grew louder ahead of them. Reaching a curving turn, the group halted and Anders motioned for the small camera to be extended.

The view from the camera showed seven Marines hunched behind barricades and raising up to fire a shot or two down the corridor at random intervals. One of the Marines had obviously overextended herself and received a hit to her faceplate that signaled her "death", so that she lay unmoving in between the two staggered barricades. Anders motioned quickly through half a dozen signals, and then waved two fingers forward.

The group sprinted around the corner, rifles raised to their shoulders so they could fire as soon as they had targets in view. Half the Marines were down before they realized an attack was coming from their rear, and the remainder turned in surprise to fire wildly at the fearsome sight of black armored assault troops advancing in lockstep. There was no mercy given, and the rest of the Marines were removed from the fight without hesitation. Group One left the stairwell to join Two, and Anders signaled for breaching charges to be placed around the locks on the door of the secure room.

After the squad retreated a few paces to either side, the charges were detonated with a quiet whump. The thick steel door was easily pushed aside by several soldiers, while other kept rifles raised to face whatever was within. Once there was enough of a crack in the doorway, flechette rounds started to pour out and clipped one of the assault soldiers standing in the firing line. The man rolled aside, his right arm dropping as the computer signaled that it had been completely disabled, his rifle clattering to the floor. The rest of the assault team found positions that let them fire at targets within the room.

"Control, Anders. We have heavy resistance within secure room. Requesting permission to use grenade, please advise."

Davis smiled tightly as he watched the action, pulling up the helmet cams from his soldiers and getting a view of the Marines within as much as possible. He would have to congratulate the leader of this squad for acting quickly to place troops inside the room instead of joining the barricades just outside. He considered the mission brief he had worked up, detailing the fact that the computer core was secure within the room but giving no information about where it might be or how exposed it could be.

"Assault team, control. Smoke grenades authorized. Repeat, smoke grenades only."

Anders tapped one of the assault troops on a shoulder, and the woman pulled a small canister from her belt. Pressing a button to arm the grenade, she tossed it through the small gap in the door. The grenade rolled loudly into the room before exploding with a flash of light. A cloud of gray smoke emitted from the canister and rapidly filled the room. Coughs could be heard within, from Marines who breathed in the thick fumes that crept under their visors and would be incapacitated for several crucial seconds.

Assault troops hurriedly pulled the door open farther and began to rush into the room, ignoring the wild shots that continued to come from within the smoke. Anders gave a verbal command and switched his HUD over to a sonar display, green outlines forming around plastic and metal objects joining yellow outlines around organic material. The squad quickly took aim on the yellow targets and fired into the smoke to drop all but one of the Marines. The last person was crouched behind a wall or partition, and the outline showed a box held in their arms that could easily be the computer core.

Anders considered the angles and sent two of his troops around the room to approach from another direction. He stepped forward and was raising his weapon when his HUD turned a blinding white for a moment before returning to a standard view. Surprised yelps from all around told him the same had happened to all of the assault squad.

"Adequate work, Ghost Squad." Davis spoke over the cargo bay speakers so the Marines could hear his words along with the assault team. "You managed to fight through most of the resistance, but the mission failed at the end. Can anyone tell me where you went wrong?"

There was silence as the assault troops looked around at each other for guidance. Davis waited, knowing that someone had to have the answer and feared voicing it and being wrong. He sent a short text to Anders that appeared in the sergeant's HUD and told him not to respond.

The Marine troops in the room and corridor began to rise to their feet with the exercise complete, most of them rubbing at bruised skin where they'd been shot. They gathered in the target room with the assault squad, waiting along the walls to watch the mission debrief.

"Sir?" Group One leader finally spoke up. "I can't think of anything we did that was wrong or against training. We had the computer core in sight. There was only one hostile left, holding it in such a way that they couldn't have pulled a weapon on us."

Davis had a camera pointed at each of the squad, watching their postures since he couldn't see faces through the dark helmets. He could see one of the youngest members of his team fidgeting, moving her weapon from one hand to another several times. "Lopez, do you have something to say?"

Her head shot up to look around at the others, and her body went tense. "We *assumed* the box held our target? Sir?"

"That is correct, Lopez. In future, don't hesitate to speak up if you have an idea. No one in this team will ridicule you if you're wrong, and I'd prefer wrong guesses to none at all." He paused to look over the team on the monitor, seeing that several of them had started to understand what happened. "The box that was being so lovingly protected by our Marine captain contained a sonic charge. Once all of the squad was within range, he hit the switch to detonate and you would all be dead had this not been an exercise."

"What? Then where was the computer core?" One of the squad called out indignantly, stepping over to lift the plastic box and look inside. He pulled out a yellow and blue canister, markings along the side to signify the sonic charge within. With disgust, he tossed the canister back in the box and set it back on the ground.

Anders started to laugh. "That was diabolical, sir."

"It was a lesson, sergeant. We are months away from seeing real action, and it's time you all learn that just because our mission targets come from the boys and girls in Intelligence, it doesn't mean that they're always correct. They can be fed bad information, or they can be working off old information where the situation is changed. Or, as in this case, you could be facing an enemy commander with the brains to realize the target objective and remove it to a place you won't think to look."

The Marine captain saluted the cameras above, and took a bow as his soldiers all started to applaud the quick-thinking action. "The computer core was dumped through to the backup system, replaced with a blank core so that even if you took me out before I could spring the trap you'd have nothing to show for it."

Anders walked over and offered a hand to the man, patting him on the shoulder as they shook. "You won this round, captain, but don't think my squad is going to fall for something like that again. We learn our lessons well, and never repeat mistakes. Right, team?"

"Yes, sergeant," they shouted out in unison.

Davis enjoyed the display of camaraderie and sent out a message to his support staff. "We have time for one more exercise. We'll take an hour break to reset the corridors and hull and see if our Marine captain can come up with more brilliant ideas to keep the next target out of our hands."

Six

Aldrin dome had been buzzing ever since the attacks in New York almost a week before. The Transport Guildhall was packed day and night in the time since, with representatives trying to get the latest news from people on Earth, while also coordinating efforts to assist the Coalition fleet with the freighters close to Luna. Outside the door, Dexterity Avila could see citizens rushing through the square at all hours. It had become a frequent occurrence for someone to dash into the hall and beg for transport back to Earth, or for transport to get family members to Luna.

She couldn't remember the last time she'd seen such visible fear on every face. When the war between the Coalition and Syndicate first broke out and raged for half a year, she'd been too young to understand what was happening. She couldn't even conjure memories of how her parents had reacted at the time, but she could imagine them feeling the same blind panic that she now witnessed every day on the streets.

The president of the Guild, Meyers, had been on Earth when the bombs in New York detonated, though on the other side of the planet in the Coalition capital of Geneva. He'd spent days meeting with a rotating cast of government ministers, trying to work out a contract to pay for the costs of his ships that were assisting the war effort. Breaking the neutrality of the Guild had been a difficult decision, but one he had deemed necessary under the circumstances. In planning to obliterate Aldrin, the Syndicate was also threatening to destroy the backbone of the Transport Guild.

He'd sent Dex messages to assure her that he and the others on the planet were safe after the bombing. The meetings had been cancelled for several days after the attack, but he was now meeting with one of the admirals near the top of the Navy's command structure. Whatever purpose had been behind the bombing, it had forced the Coalition leadership to react with more urgency to the threats they were facing.

In his absence, Dex was nominally in charge of the Guildhall. She felt herself being pulled in a hundred different directions every moment, with reps calling for her input or approval several times every minute. By the end of each day, she was so exhausted that she never managed to call her parents or check in with Nat on the *Waterloo*.

"Dex," a man called from two desks away. "We have a transport shuttle docking at Armstrong with a dozen crates marked for delivery to the Hall. Should I head over and escort them in?"

"Yeah, Rex, go handle that. If it's the shipment I'm expecting, that's the extra servers and routers we need to connect with the Coalition networks." She watched the man rush out, and sighed when his terminal started beeping insistently a moment later with more incoming calls.

She answered half a dozen calls, most of them video messages from freighter captains asking if they should continue on with their contracts. In every instance, she followed Meyers' directives and confirmed that they should return to Luna immediately. It was hard for a freighter captain to turn away from a contract, especially when so many ran on the razor edge of not being able to pay for their ship's upkeep.

When she got a video call from Earth, she answered it excitedly. "How'd the meeting go, sir?"

"They tried to haggle us down to a bare minimum contract," Meyers told her, a wide smile on his face. "I put my decades of negotiation experience to work, though, and got us five percent more than I expected. Let our captains know that as of this moment, everyone is getting paid daily rates. We are under contract for two years, or the end of the conflict with the Syndicate. Whichever comes first."

Dex relaxed her tense shoulders and pumped a fist in the air. "That is great news! We have seven ships confirmed to be burning for Luna now. Three captains are two weeks or less from their destinations, and will head for Luna after a fast unload."

"What about the other nine?"

"One of those is the *Vagabond.* They seem to be heading back to Luna based on the messages I've received, but Captain Frost still has his eye on that cruiser and could veer off to follow them at any moment." Dex shook her head, frustrated that the man kept trying to throw himself into dangerous situations. "Six ships have responded to our recall requests with questions or complaints that they haven't delivered cargo. Two haven't responded yet. I'm reaching out to them all to emphasize the importance of returning."

"Excellent job, Dex. Keep me updated if any of them give you problems. Remind them that we have the ability to pull their Guild licenses, if you have to." Meyers looked away from the screen, and nodded at someone she couldn't see. "Next meeting is starting in five. I'm trying to convince the Admiralty that our ships need weapons. If we can add some firepower to the fleet, maybe we can help even the odds a little."

"Good luck, sir." Dex tapped the button to end the call and turned her attention back to the chaos around her. There were three people already calling for her attention as soon as they saw she was off the call.

By the time she was able to step away from the hall and take a break, Dex was surprised to find that it was late afternoon already. It had been more than four hours since the call with President Meyers, and she knew the meetings would be wrapping for the day soon. Like almost every part of Earth, Geneva followed System Standard time. Even though it would be the middle of the solar night on their part of the planet, the large majority of the workforce would be ending their work day and heading home.

Dex grabbed a quick meal at a noodle shop a block from the square. Slurping up lo mein, she kept an eye on the small screen inset on the counter in front of her. Security forces were still investigating the New York bombings, but were finally releasing the official count of dead and missing. Eight and a half thousand people gone in the blink of an eye, with several thousand more still hospitalized. The scale of the attack was staggering.

She was popping the last chunk of chicken-flavored tofu into her mouth when her tablet started to buzz at her elbow. Dex waved at the cook behind the counter as she pushed the bowl away. She turned on the stool and answered the incoming call as she left the noodle shop.

"Dex, please tell me you want to come down here and take my place." Meyers looked much more haggard than he had earlier in the day.

"Meetings aren't going well, sir?"

"I feel like I'm a ball being bounced between several different people. And they keep throwing me with more force than the time before." He wiped a hand over his face. She could see the background bouncing slightly, and knew he was walking somewhere. "The Admiralty seems amenable to arming our freighters with light railguns, but the Defense Minister is adamant that we would have to sign on to the Coalition charter before it could be allowed."

"If we did that, our captains would take their ships and go independent again. Do they really want that to happen?"

"It didn't turn out very well before the Guild, and I can't see it working any better in the middle of an escalating war. We're meeting again tomorrow, so hopefully after some rest I can convince…"

The feed distorted, as if the signal was buffering, and then her screen went dark for a second. The tablet's main menu appeared, and Dex stopped in the middle of the street to frown at the device. She tapped at the button to call her boss back, but got a message that the network was unavailable. The connection was fine with the Luna network, which she tested by pulling up a few celebrity gossip websites that she usually visited in bed at night to relax her brain.

A scream from the direction of the square drew her attention, followed by yells and other noises. She jogged toward the Guildhall and entered to find the long room eerily quiet and still. The representatives and visitors were all huddled around displays on the desks.

"…explosions occurred minutes ago, at 17.08 System Standard. All we know at this time is that there were two simultaneous detonations. One was in or near the main Coalition government building complex, and the second was at the Geneva transport hub and spaceport. We have been unable to reach any of our reporters in the area, but will continue…"

Dex felt the blood drain from her body.

Seven

Nat watched from a service catwalk high above as a clean slate-gray shuttle slowly entered the docking bay. With gentle puffs of thrust, the pilot set the shuttle down in the exact center of the illuminated landing area. A group in dress uniforms with tassels and gold braid approached the shuttle, the command staff of the *Waterloo* with her captain at the fore. When the ramp of the shuttle opened with a hiss of air and began to drop on silent hydraulics, the officers stiffened and hands snapped to their temples in salutes that they held until occupants of the shuttle began to emerge.

The first person to exit was a man in his sixties wearing a crisp white uniform, his chest covered in medals and insignia, displaying a long and distinguished career in the Navy that had seen him rise to the rank of Fleet Admiral. Behind were two commanders, a man in his late forties and a woman that looked to be a decade younger. Both returned the salutes of the ship's command staff, and Captain Andrews stepped forward to shake hands with the admiral.

"Sir, it is an honor to have you aboard. Thank you for choosing the *Waterloo* to carry your flag in the coming confrontation."

"Captain," the admiral acknowledged, stepping off the ramp with the captain following beside him while the commanders were only steps behind. "You've done well with the retrofitting and upgrades. My aides didn't expect you to complete them within the schedule."

“Two days early, sir,” the captain said with pride. “My Engineering team is the best in the fleet, and the help from the shipyards was a nice bump to speed things along. The weapons tests earlier this week show a ninety-eight percent efficiency rate on the new railguns and torpedo launchers.”

“Excellent news, captain. Your old weapons are already being delivered to the shipyards on Luna to be installed on the Guild freighters. I anticipate using their ships in support roles where needed.”

The words faded as the party passed through the doors and out of the docking bay. Nat watched as the pilot and steward of the admiral’s shuttle exited the craft to begin checking over the shiny plastic-looking hull. She shook her head over the vanity of people at the top who thought nothing of spending tens of thousands of credits to apply a glossy coating over steel plates on a shuttle that was rarely used, but would then balk at a five thousand credit request for needed repairs on a frigate. The shuttle pilot pulled a cloth from his pocket and rubbed at a spot on the short wing, examining the cloth in between to look at whatever dirt or residue was coming off.

Rolling her eyes, Nat pushed off from the railing she’d been leaning on and walked a few steps to enter the bay control room. Two people were ensconced in comfortable chairs, their hands and eyes darting across screens as they monitored and controlled the operations within the bay as well as the personnel and cargo shuttles that were entering and exiting. The flight path had been cleared for more than an hour to allow a smooth flight for the admiral’s shuttle, and they were scrambling now to get back on schedule with the day's deliveries. A battered old cargo hauler was entering the bay already, the cheap paint on the hull blistered and blackened from repeated re-entries through Earth's atmosphere.

"Nat, what brings you to my little kingdom?" The man who spoke was rail thin, with thick brown hair that stuck up in all directions as if it had never been touched by a comb. He smiled at her from where he stood behind the two crewmembers directing traffic around the bay.

"Lieutenant Simon, sir," she replied with a grin, throwing a quick salute. The *Waterloo*'s docking bay was one of her frequent haunts, the chief engineer sending her to handle most of the maintenance and repair requests. There were many for the most heavily trafficked area of the ship, especially over the last few months with new parts coming in and old parts leaving the ship every day. "Chief said one of the freight arms is giving you guys a bit of trouble?"

"Ah, yes! I'd forgotten all about that with the admiral coming in. It's the one over in C-5, where we keep overflow when the main cargo area is full."

"I'll get on it," she promised, glancing around the docking bay as she spoke. With the command staff and admiral no longer inhibiting them, the crew below were hurrying to complete their assigned tasks. Many of them eyed the spotless shuttle with disdain. She could hear one of the controllers speaking with someone requesting to have the shuttle moved out of the way so carts could get to the cargo shuttle that had just completed a landing mostly within its own illuminated area. "Going to be a busy day, sir?"

“We already have to figure out how to fit twelve hours of work into an eight hour shift. Now we need to do it in seven.”

“That’s it? You slackers have it easy. Try working in Engineering sometime.” She smiled at the frazzled officer, saluting again as she turned and left the busy room to get to work on repairing the crane arm. She grabbed up her diagnostic and tool kit from where she had watched the admiral’s arrival, and waved at several people she recognized below as she traversed the catwalks to get to the C-5 cargo niche. Sliding down a ladder to a lower catwalk, she approached the crane controls and pulled a screwdriver to pop open the panel and check the wiring first.

While she worked, Nat thought back over the last couple of weeks. The memories were mostly a haze of work and exhaustion, even when she had been given a few days off after completing the retrofitting, before they started running tests on all the new systems and weapon emplacements.

The bombing in New York had occupied the conversation on the ship for several days, and the only good news to come out of it was that Janet’s parents had finally been able to get in touch and let her know they were okay and had left the city after the bombing to stay with friends for a while. When several days had dragged on with no indication of which person or group was responsible for the attack, the conversation around it turned to complaints and recriminations against the security forces on Earth that were investigating.

When another set of bombs detonated in Geneva four days after New York, it was a staggering event for the crew of the ship as much as the people on the planet. Government officials had been meeting in the city to discuss the approach of the Syndicate cruiser and the earlier bombings, trying to decide if the events were related or just a case of someone being crazy enough to create more chaos for the hell of it. The prime minister had not been able to make the meeting, sending his deputy prime minister instead along with half a dozen of his cabinet. All of them had been killed in the blast, which destroyed the foundations of the eighty-story building and caused it to collapse only minutes later. Almost four thousand people died in that attack, sending the Coalition into a deeper mourning and increasing the calls for answers.

Nat had spent hours talking with her parents and her sister in the days after the second bombing. Her mother was growing more worried for her daughters, almost begging Dex to get off Luna and return to their home near Mexico City. Dex resisted, insisting that she was doing important work with the Transport Guild on Luna that would lead to large contributions to the coming battle between the two navies.

When they spoke without their parents on the call, Dex confided that half of the Guild's administrative staff had fled back to Earth as they became more and more convinced that the Syndicate cruiser couldn't be stopped and would destroy Aldrin dome with little or no resistance from the Coalition frigates still hovering protectively over the home world. Nat herself had lost all concern about being aboard a warship, feeling a need to contribute however she could to stop people who would kill innocent civilians by the thousands. Like most of her crewmates, she had little doubt that the Syndicate was behind the terrorist bombings.

Then, two weeks to the day after the first attacks, a bomb went off in Monaco. The small nation had retained its independence, resisting the pressures that had forced all but a few of the old Earth countries to join either the Coalition or Syndicate decades before. It was surrounded by Coalition territory, but served as an exclusive vacation destination for the wealthier citizens of both superpowers. The high-class Monte Carlo casino, more than two hundred years old, had been the target of the bomb. The Coalition prime minister's wife had been staying in an adjacent hotel, gambling the nights away with her friends. It was pure luck that she'd happened to visit a nightclub several blocks away on the evening that the bombs were set off. More than seven hundred were killed in the explosion. The centuries-old casino building was all but obliterated, and the attack on an independent nation had started a howl of dismay and anger even from within Syndicate territory.

It also finally hardened the resolve of the Coalition government and military commanders. Emergency measures were pushed through the houses of parliament to award a hefty budget increase, and all resistance to arming the Guild freighters was wiped away. A proposal to immediately begin construction on two more frigates, the most their orbital station shipyard could handle at once, was also passed and the funds set aside. Everyone involved knew it would take most of a year to complete the projects, but agreed to it for the sake of being seen to do something about the increasing threat.

Two small fighters had been loaded into the docking bay of the *Waterloo*. They were secured high above, out of the way of day-to-day activities but able to be quickly readied in the event that their pilots were called to scramble into cockpits and launch from the ship. Five squads of Marines had been added to the ship, sharing crowded cabins and training areas with the five squads that had already been permanently stationed aboard the frigate. All the arms and armor for the additional forty Marines also had to be stuffed into packed storage rooms. The frigate was bursting at the seams, and every other frigate in the fleet was similarly overloaded.

Nat finished the repairs on the freight crane, running it through a few tests to ensure the movement was free and easy before checking it off on her duty schedule and sending a message to let the chief engineer know the work was complete. She was halfway through her shift, and working the kinds of jobs she enjoyed most. After almost two months of long hours and hectic work in tight service tunnels, going back to working a normal shift felt like a vacation. Leaving the docking bay behind, she smiled and whistled softly as she headed aft to handle the next service request.

EIGHT

"It's only been two weeks since Geneva, and now there's been a third bomb attack in Monaco. They still don't know who's doing it or how they're getting the explosives so close to important buildings. It has to be the Syndicate, right?"

"Maybe, but what would they gain from it? The system knows about their cruiser now, that it destroyed the colony on Interamnia and plans to do the same on Mars and Luna. A few bombs on Earth aren't going to make people forget that."

"No, but it will take their main focus away from a threat that's a few months away at best to one that's more immediate. The Coalition frigates still haven't moved from their orbit over Earth, and they've even called Marines down to the planet to help with the security around the three attack sites."

Erik was leaning against a bulkhead down the corridor from the galley, listening to the discussion. The news of the first attack in New York City had left him stunned, and a second attack less than a week later in Geneva was like a hammer blow. Terrorist attacks like these had been somewhat common at the beginning of the twenty-first century, but it had been decades since they had been carried out on such a large scale. Coalition government buildings and officials were the obvious targets, but the bombers also aimed for maximum casualties with each blast.

He walked into the galley to join Isaac, Tom and Fynn. He nodded as he passed the table to get a cup of coffee, and then joined them after grabbing a meal bar. "The attacks, huh?"

"I can't understand why anyone would do something so destructive," Isaac said. "If they're targeting the Coalition government, why kill so many innocents?"

"Because that's what gets the headlines," Fynn replied cynically. "If it *is* the Syndicate behind the bombs, then they want the average citizen of the Coalition to be afraid to leave their homes. Make them stay home, strangle trade and spending, and you hurt the government just as much as you would if you killed the prime minister himself. With the cruiser approaching Earth, and the war ramping up for the first time in decades, they're going to need all the credits they can get from taxes."

Tom still looked unconvinced. "I spent most of seven years on that warship, working alongside crew and soldiers in the Syndicate Navy. I can't imagine any of them being happy about these bombings and all the people that are being killed."

"They didn't seem to mind targeting civilians on the colonies and Luna. Not to mention the cities they plan to bombard from orbit." Erik clenched his jaw, wanting to lash out in anger at the man for daring to think anything but the worst about the people who had killed his friends.

"I can't deny that," Tom said with a grimace.

"You'll both understand better when you get to be my age," Fynn asserted, running a hand through his rapidly graying hair. "It's all about the perspective. If you're working on a ship that fired the blast that destroyed a colony, you don't feel involved because you're removed from the people who actually fired the weapons."

"And if you fired the weapons, you don't feel responsible because you were just following orders." Erik shook his head, but couldn't refute it. "On and on, all the way up to the Executive Committee that rules the Syndicate and gave the orders to begin the construction of the cruiser."

Tom thought about that for a second and then snorted in agreement. "I talked to one of the Marine soldiers who executed my friends once and asked him how he could live with it. The guy gave me the most baffled look, said he was just following orders. If his sergeant told him to shoot someone, then the higher ups had to have an excellent reason for wanting it done."

Fynn nodded. "Militaries have been built on structures of discipline and following orders for centuries. Soldiers are trained to do what they're told, and never to question it. When there *are* abuses, it's almost always the people at the top of the command chain responsible for it." He paused for a moment. "Of course, the people below sometimes feel the same prejudices or desires to punish what they see as unjust restrictions on their people. That's been responsible for some of the worst atrocities on Earth the last several hundred years."

"Okay, but what about the bombings?" Isaac asked. "If it's the Syndicate, why isn't the Coalition doing something to stop it?"

"There's nothing they can do until they find out who's responsible," Erik told him. "I'd like to know why they haven't sent any ships after the Syndicate frigates that are close to rendezvousing with the cruiser. If they'd acted quickly, they could have intercepted at least a few of them to prevent supplies and more crew from reaching the *Indomitable*."

"Inertia," Fynn complained. "The Coalition government was too accustomed to decades of verbal sparring. That was the extent of hostilities in the cold war. They didn't realize quickly enough that the other side had decided to ramp up the aggression with no warning."

"It's been over a month, Fynn. They still haven't moved their eight frigates except to cluster them close to Earth."

"I'm sure the Fleet Admiral and his staff have been working on strategies to counter the Syndicate ships when they get closer. We just won't know what that is until it happens."

Erik was grumbling discontentedly as Mira poked her head into the room. "Cap, got a message for you from Luna. It came in with Guild recognition codes. It has the highest encryption I've ever seen."

"Coming," he said, rising to put his cup in the sanitizer and leave the others to continue their discussion. Following Mira to the control center, he tried to force the frustration of apparent Coalition inaction from his mind. He slid into his command chair and the holo display flickered to life in front of him showing the message queued up for his authorization codes. Typing them in with deft strokes, he watched the screen flash as the message opened. President Meyers, head of the Transport Guild, appeared on screen.

Erik felt a spike of elation. Dex had shared her concerns about Meyers being in Geneva during the bombings, and it was good to see that the man had made it through. He knew that Dex must be glad of the enormous weight off her shoulders.

"Captain Frost, I know Dexterity expressed her concerns for me after the Geneva bombings. I was in between the government center and transport hub, spared the worst of both explosions. I'll have a few bumps and bruises to remind me of the event for a while longer, but I made it through okay.

Excellent work getting one of those Syndicate railguns installed on your ship. I'm sure we can get the second mounted with the help of the Luna shipyards at a later date. As you may know, I have been in contact with the Coalition government to coordinate our efforts against the Syndicate threat." Erik had to shake his head and smile in bemusement at how the man fell into political speech even in a private message, using words that seemingly downplayed the danger they were facing.

"The prime minister and I are in agreement that our fleets will work better together rather than facing the incoming cruiser alone. To that end, I have acquired permission and funding to arm all of our freighters with light railguns, and will be starting to get them into the shipyards for retrofitting as slips become available. I'd like the *Vagabond* to change course to meet with a ship that is returning from the colony on Hygeia, the *Tamerlane*. Escort her to Luna, and then join the combined fleet of Coalition frigates and Guild freighters. Our latest estimates show that you should arrive ahead of the Syndicate cruiser if it continues on course to stop at Mars before proceeding to Earth.

"Thank you again for providing warnings of the existence of the cruiser, Captain Frost. The system owes you a debt that I hope we are able to pay when this is all resolved." With those words, the screen went black and the message closed. Coordinates were thrown up on the screen for the recommended rendezvous point with the *Tamerlane*, and Erik ran a few projections on the course needed to meet the other freighter. If he could push both ships a little harder, they should still arrive on Luna around the same projected day of their current course, but he had already been pushing the *Vagabond* harder than he liked. They still had weak hull plates on the bow, with every hard burn putting pressure on them.

Transferring the coordinates to the main display, he rose and walked over to lean on the pilot's console. "We've been requested to re-route to those coordinates to meet with another freighter, and then escort them to Luna. Do what you can to try and shave some time off the detour."

"Will do, cap. Does this mean we're going to miss the action?"

"Not if I can help it. Sounds like the government has decided to let the Syndicate have their way with Mars. I don't agree with that decision at all, but with the positioning of the planets that will add a few weeks to their trip and allow us to shoot past and reach Luna before they can."

"There's a couple of hundred scientists on Mars, along with a hundred more people on the Deimos outpost. They're just going to let those people get killed without raising a finger?"

Erik shrugged angrily. "The prime minister is going to have a lot to answer for when this is all done, assuming the Syndicate doesn't succeed in their plans."

Shaking her head in disbelief, Mira started running course adjustment calculations and Erik left the control room to walk to his cabin. He wanted privacy for the next message he planned to send. Sitting at the small desk near his bunk, he turned on the display and started recording.

"Dex, I just got the message from Meyers. It's good to see him, and I know you have to be overjoyed that he survived the attacks in Geneva." He sighed heavily. "Any word from your sources about the research I forwarded from Robert? He sounded like he was close to a breakthrough before Interamnia was destroyed, and now that we have several people looking into it I was hoping they could get over whatever hurdles he encountered. That new power source could give us a real boost against the Syndicate fleet in a few months when it approaches Earth and Luna. Make sure you take care of yourself, Dex. Don't push yourself too hard."

Tapping a few buttons, Erik encrypted the message and sent it to the Luna relays. He leaned back in his chair and reflected on how chaotic the system had gotten over the last six weeks since his escape from the *Indomitable.* He felt better knowing his ship had a heavy railgun mounted above the hastily repaired bow, but wished they had been able to get the second onto the belly of the ship.

Fynn said that mounting the gun there would require cutting into the hull and rerouting a lot of conduits, which couldn't be done while the ship was hurrying to get back to Luna. Considering that the Syndicate container had only included several dozen depleted uranium rounds to use in the railguns, he knew that a second weapon would be of very limited benefit until they could get a larger stock of ammunition.

If they encountered a Syndicate frigate alone, they would stand no chance and would be lucky to get off a few shots. But if they could join a small fleet of freighters carrying light railguns, then they could match up against a frigate or two and help in a fight alongside the Coalition fleet. It was his only hope to fight back and try to get some measure of revenge for the deaths of the Murphys and everyone else on Interamnia. He just didn't know if it would be enough to assuage the guilt he felt for kickstarting the cruiser on its mission.

NINE

Tuya banged her head against the bulkhead she was leaning on, roaring in frustration. For two months she'd been stuck aboard the *Indomitable*, and for six of those weeks she'd known where her brother was being held but been unable to reach him. She watched shift changes for days, passed by in the early morning hours when few people could claim not to be tired near the end of an overnight shift, and even engaged one Marine in a bit of conversation. She could find no gaps in the security that she'd be able to exploit on her own, and the frustration was getting to her more and more every day.

She had managed to get a tablet, finding a crate of them in a dusty storage room that was obviously forgotten somewhere along the way. It was loaded up with old software, at least six months out of date, but allowed her to access the cruiser's network and pull down censored news reports that were vetted and approved for viewing by the crew. Most of the reports and videos were propaganda pieces. One was blaming the Coalition for food shortages in one part of the Syndicate's Asian territory, while another story praised citizens in South America for exceeding production goals for their sector.

Reports about the bombings on Earth had been almost gleeful. The thousands of deaths were trumpeted as cosmic justice against the people who'd been trying for so long to stop the Syndicate from reaching their full potential. Government officials talked to reporters about how the

Coalition's inability to protect their citizens was a sign of their weakness and ineptitude. The head of the Military Committee made light of the deaths. She said it was the fault of the Coalition security forces for growing lax over the years and failing to provide proper training that would allow their personnel to identify and trace such threats.

After the attack on Monaco, the trillionaire owner of a technology company who was a member of the ruling Executive Committee held a press conference. He announced that a handful of victims had been Syndicate citizens. He railed at the Coalition leadership for failing to identify the bomber or bombers in the two weeks since the first attack, and put the blame for his citizens' deaths squarely on the Coalition leadership. The one thing everyone refused to do was take credit for the attacks, or even intimate that the Syndicate might be behind them.

Tuya couldn't see news reports from within the Coalition, so she had no idea what the true casualty counts might be or where their investigations might have taken them so far. Her only consolation was that her parents, living in northern Mongolia and close to the border between the two superpowers, were far from heavily populated areas that provided tempting targets for such a terror campaign. Thinking of her parents only made her realize how much she missed them, and how little hope she had of escaping the *Indomitable* to ever see them again.

Shaking off the melancholy and frustration, Tuya tried to formulate a new plan. If she couldn't find a gap in the security to exploit, perhaps there was another course of action that would allow her to get to her brother. She knew the Syndicate frigates were growing nearer, and had seen the alerts on her tablet about preparing to receive reinforcements. Conceivably there could be a way to take advantage of the influx of new people to the ship. When there were strange faces all around, one more would be easy to miss.

Resolved to a course of action, she set about polishing the stolen Marine armor to a glossy black shine. Walking the halls with armor in less than perfect condition would be a sure way to attract attention that she didn't want. Strapping on the pieces once she was done, she pulled up duty rosters on the tablet and created a mental map of the best route to her destination.

Pulling the helmet over her head, Tuya exited the storage closet that had been her latest home for a few days and strode down the corridor. It was the second hour of the morning, and the hallways were barren. Most of the people awake at this time were on duty throughout the ship, minimizing the possibility of running into anyone not rushing to get a job done.

Marines usually patrolled the ship in pairs. Walking alone in the armor was a constant risk even now that they often patrolled alone due to the reduced number of troops available for each shift. She had stuck with wearing the armor only because of the helmet visor that kept all but her mouth obscured, and the armor plating that made it harder for observers to guess her size. There were cameras throughout the ship's corridors, but few of them were monitored on a consistent basis.

The number of Marines on board was far below the required number for a ship this size, especially after she and the others had killed almost a dozen during the *Vagabond's* escape. Because of that, those who were on duty were often so overworked that they tended to snap and assault crew members who stepped out of line. That led to few of the crew feeling a desire to pay close attention when they saw a Marine walking down the hallway for fear of drawing her ire.

It took more than an hour to reach her destination, traveling several miles through corridors and stairwells on a roundabout path that was designed to keep her away from busy areas of the ship. Entering the small engineering sub-station near the main hangar and docking bay, Tuya made a quick survey of the room and verified that she was alone. She crossed to the storage lockers, and shoved aside tools and diagnostic kits until she found what she had been searching for. Crumpled at the bottom of one of the lockers was a grease-covered red jumpsuit, the name patch on the chest faded and stained from dozens of shifts. She felt sure that whoever it belonged to wouldn't miss the garment, and shoved the wadded jumpsuit under her chest armor where it could rest unseen.

Tuya pulled a few tools from the locker, and a small portable diagnostic scanning device that looked well used. She knew older items were missed less frequently, and if someone did go looking they would probably be glad to take the opportunity to requisition a newer replacement. Secreting the tools and scanner under her armor, she tried to return the lockers to the condition they had been in prior to her search, and then closed them tightly.

Leaving the room, she tried to ignore the lumpy feeling of the wadded jumpsuit pushing against her breasts, pulling on the armor now and then in an attempt to shift the garment into a more comfortable position.

There was a tense moment as she saw a Marine patrol approaching down a long corridor. She considered ducking through a nearby door, but knew that would draw suspicion. Instead, she took advantage of her earlier movements and started to cough loudly. Continuing to pull and push on the chest plate, she added in a pained moan as the patrol got closer and coughed louder.

"You need to get that checked out," one of the Marines said, as the pair stopped. One of their helmets was lowered, and she realized that the extra padding from the jumpsuit pushed out her chest armor and made her bust look larger.

"Yeah, on the way to medical now," Tuya replied hoarsely, trying to disguise her voice as much as possible.

"We're headed to the bar on deck 18 after shift, if you want to stop in," the second Marine said, with a leering smile barely visible under the faceplate of the helmet.

"Maybe, have to see what the doc says." She waved and walked on, holding her breath and listening as hard as she could to see if they would follow or continue on their patrol.

"That had to be Saunders. She's the only one with tits that big." The words were barely audible as the patrol turned and continued in the opposite direction.

Tuya snarled and clenched her hands, wishing she could have slapped the irritating smile from the Marine's face and taught them both to respect the women they served with. It also made her nervous to think that her cover might be blown. If they asked this Saunders person about her throat, or mentioned meeting in the corridor, then a denial would lead them to wonder who she could have been since no one else apparently matched her very padded build.

She reflected that this might be the last time it would be safe to walk the halls in Marine armor, since they may all be on higher alert looking for an explanation of who the patrol met. Her only hope was that the men would get drunk after shift and forget all about it, or that their possible report would be dismissed when no one could be found to corroborate it.

Checking the map on her tablet, she found a long stretch of empty cabins that had not yet been allocated for the soon-to-arrive additions. She traveled up two decks and across to the port side of the cruiser without seeing another person, and entered one of the cabins. Like every other cabin she'd spent time in over the last few months, it looked almost exactly the same as the room she had been imprisoned in with her friends. That imprisonment had lasted less than a day for her, but she knew that she would never forget the helpless feeling. It had been that more than anything else that drove her to hold out in the abusive interrogation, and over the last two months as she worked to free her brother from his cell.

Stripping out of the armor pieces, she stuffed them into a drawer and examined the jumpsuit she had stolen. It was made for someone half a head taller and a couple of dozen pounds heavier, but luckily the basic crew of every ship in the system preferred wearing loose garments as a way to reinforce that they weren't as confined by rules as the tightly uniformed military officers and troops they had to serve with.

Tossing the stained jumpsuit into the sanitizer, she took the opportunity to peel off the biosuit that she'd been wearing for most of the last two months and add it in, as well. Feeling free now that the skintight suit was no longer constricting her, Tuya entered the shower and spent half an hour getting spritzed with hot water from the dozens of jets and luxuriating in the cleanliness of rubbing fresh smelling soap over her arms, legs, and torso. She washed her hair for the first time in weeks, relishing the feel of her fingers running through the black locks that were now long enough to fall below her shoulders.

Clean and refreshed, she wrapped herself in a soft towel and threw herself onto one of the bunks in the room. She tried to remember how many nights she'd spent on a mattress during her extended stay on the cruiser, and could only decide it had been few enough to count on one hand. Hiding in storage rooms was always a safer option, with a very low risk of having someone enter unexpectedly to prepare the room for use. She silently thanked whoever left the jumpsuit in the locker for not bothering to clean it first, giving her the excuse to spend some in a cabin.

Lying on her back, Tuya closed her eyes and listened to the throb of the ship around her. The constant firing of the ion thrusters as the cruiser pushed itself farther into the system generated a steady hum that had become comforting to her. It reminded her of the rattling old claptrap of a freighter she had spent four years living on, wonderful thoughts that soothed her and sent her into happy dreams of days spent with a crew that had felt like family.

TEN

Erik watched as the *Tamerlane* approached, growing larger in the view from the bow cameras. The two freighters were on courses that would bring them within fifty kilometers of each other for the remainder of the journey to Luna. He had met the captain of the other Guild ship a few times when their paths crossed, and while the man was haughty and imperious he could also be generous and charitable with his friends.

"Frost," the other captain said curtly when he answered the communications request from the *Vagabond.* "Looks like that old trash hauler of yours has grown a horn."

Erik chuckled in agreement. "A horn that's ready to gore some Syndicate ships. How are you doing, Farouk?"

"We were doing very good until this urgent summons back to Luna. I was just loading up a couple of cargo pods to deliver out to the mining colony on Davida. That would have put us in the green for this trip to the belt. Now I'll be carrying them around to no purpose and no pay." The large black eyebrows drew in over chocolate brown eyes, a line of frustration forming between them.

"If we don't manage to stop this Syndicate cruiser, then there'll be no more profits for any of us. Or ships to captain, I imagine."

"Yes, so President Meyers says in his message that tells me to run back to mama." The middle-aged captain snorted and waved a hand through the air. "They will put some small pea shooter railgun on my baby, and then send me to fight against frigates? What sense does this make?"

"You won't be fighting alone," Erik said. "Hopefully, most of the Guild ships will be armed by the time the cruiser approaches Earth. We'll also be fighting alongside the Coalition frigates."

"Give me a strong gun like the one I see on your ship, and I would feel like my *Tamerlane* had a chance in a battle. These old light railguns they are handing out to us were designed for days when pirates in ships older than our freighters were the only enemy to worry about."

"I wish I had some of them to hand out. We were lucky to get two of them, but not lucky enough to have enough rounds to make them more than a minor nuisance for the Syndicate fleet."

Farouk clenched his jaw, and then his expression softened on the holo display. "I am sorry to hear about John and Sally. I did not know them well, but always there were good things said about them."

"They're sorely missed," Erik replied softly.

"Is it true that this Syndicate cruiser killed all of the colonists on Interamnia?"

"Their weapons tore the asteroid apart, Farouk. The cavern where the colony was set up is gone, and the mining tunnels must have funneled the blast in such a way that it split Interamnia into hundreds of pieces. The bulk of the asteroid is still there, but it's seventy percent of what it used to be."

"Never did I think I would see such butchery." Farouk slammed a fist on his chair. "What is the universe coming to when people with such barbaric ideas are given command of ships? It pains me that the nation I was born to is part of the Syndicate."

"That's why it's imperative we do everything in our power to fight back and stop them." Erik said. He turned and looked at the terminal to his right, eyes darting across the numbers displayed. He wondered about the best approach to get what he wanted from the other captain. "Can your freighter manage a fifteen minute six G acceleration burn four times a day, with a thrust of one third G in between?"

"No! You are pushing your ship too hard if that is what you have been doing. Our babies must be cared for. Nurtured. Treated like the queens of our hearts." The old captain placed a hand tenderly on his chest as he spoke. "I will do this hard burn two times each day, but I protest it every time."

"Protest it as much as you like, as long as you do it." Erik smiled into the camera to take the bite out of his words. "I want to beat that cruiser to Earth, and if you can give me the acceleration burn twice a day we can arrive at Luna in a little over three weeks according to my projections. That should be almost a month ahead of their long detour to Mars."

The connection was ended, and Erik turned off the holo display to rise from his command chair. "Work out a schedule for the burns with the pilot of the *Tamerlane*," he told Mira. "We also need to figure out when to start the braking burns. I'm guessing we'll need at least a week to shed off our speed before reaching Luna."

"More than that, cap." Mira turned her chair to look at him. "We've built up so much speed that my calculations are calling for nine days of hard braking burns. I'll see if the other freighter is sturdy enough for that, but if not we might want to start them two weeks out from Luna."

Erik groaned at the thought. "How much does that push back our arrival?"

"A couple of days," the pilot said with a shrug. "Four at the most."

"Okay, do whatever you think best for *Vagabond.* I trust your judgement." Leaving the control room, he marveled at the words he'd just spoken. It had been only two months since he met Mira, but already he felt as comfortable with her at the controls of his ship as he had when John Murphy sat in the chair. Stressful situations had bred a quick camaraderie in the combined crew, to the point that it was hard to think of them as separate crews anymore. They were all part of the *Vagabond* now.

With those thoughts in his head, he altered his planned course, turning right instead of left. Entering the cargo bay, he looked around the space and felt a wave of nostalgia for all the days he had shared with Tuya there. He reached out to pat one of the cargo pods they had picked up on Interamnia, a last remnant of the destroyed colony. The analytical part of his brain wondered who would get paid for the load of ores and minerals now that the colony no longer existed, but he shoved that down with ease.

Erik found the person he was looking for farther inside the bay, hunched over a scattering of armor pieces that had been black when brought aboard the freighter. Tom was working on scouring the surface of the lightweight metal to strip the black paint and expose the dull gray surface beneath. It took days of hard work to get the enamel layer removed, heating it and then scrubbing at it before heating it again.

"Looks like you only have a few bits left," Erik said as he bent to pick up a completely stripped forearm plate.

"Captain," Tom said, not looking up from where he was rubbing a rough wire pad in constant strokes.

Erik watched him work for a minute, feeling bad for neglecting the man who had not only lost his ship and most of his fellow crew seven years before, but then had his best friend turn against them during the escape from the *Indomitable*. Aside from the day they'd all met in the galley to talk through their feelings of loss and anger, he had rarely taken a moment to get to know Tom. Mira he saw every day, and Jen he spoke with at least a couple of times each week as they bumped into each other in the galley or when she was giving updates on any medical treatments that had been required.

"How are things going in the engine room?"

"Good. Fynn and I get along really well." Tom had been spending most of his days working with the engineer or on the hull repairs and railgun emplacement with the old Norwegian.

"You've been doing great work down there. Thanks for putting in so much time to help get the ship ready for whatever comes."

Tom scrubbed at the armor for a few more strokes, and then set the wire pad aside and looked up to meet Erik's eyes. "Did you have something you wanted to talk about?"

"I just want to check in and make sure you're doing okay. I haven't taken the time to speak with you much since the *Indomitable*. You saved us back there, and I hope you know how much we all appreciate it."

"Tuya saved us," the former Marine said. "I couldn't even see that Richard was going to double cross us before it happened, even though I saw all the signs."

Sighing, Erik crouched down to be on the same level. "We all have a blindness to the failings of the people we care about. Don't be hard on yourself for not seeing it. Jen said she noticed the same signs you did. Richard spending more time with friends outside of the old *Telemachus* crew, and seeming to be more comfortable under the Syndicate military discipline than in the earlier years. She didn't think he would turn on his old crew, either."

"Yeah, but I'm the one who spent almost every day by his side." Tom tossed the shin armor to the ground in disgust. "We walked patrols for hours on end, we nursed our small daily alcohol allowance in bars after shifts, we even shared the same cabin."

“There you go.” Erik shrugged and held out his hands. “You were with him every day, more than anyone, too close to see the wider view. It’s like a problem in the engine room. You know there’s some malfunction in the wiring somewhere, you spend hours sorting through everything that you felt could be the problem, and then someone else comes in and spots the problem in ten minutes. They’re looking at the problem with a fresh perspective, without all the built-in biases and assumptions that everyone develops when they’re around things all the time.”

“I still should have seen it.” Tom shook his head, and turned his eyes away. “If I had just spoken up about some of the things I’d seen, maybe all of us would have seen the danger.”

“What then?” Erik asked, an eyebrow raised.

“Then we wouldn’t have been betrayed!”

“How would you have accomplished that? Leave Richard out of the plan? Leave him behind on the *Indomitable* instead?”

“Yeah, if we had to. At least then I wouldn’t have to keep reliving that instant in the hallway when he turned against us. I dream of that moment every night. When I can sleep at all.”

Erik reached out a hand to grab at Tom’s arm. “You would have traded one regret for another, that’s all. You’d be dreaming of leaving Richard behind, always wondering if he would’ve really turned on you or joined in the escape plan after all. There was no way to come out of that situation with a win, but there’s also no reason to continue blaming yourself for something that should be solely laid at Richard's feet. It was his decision to turn his back on family."

Tom slammed a fist against the floor and growled. "I know that. I hate Richard for what he did, the way he betrayed everything we'd built up from the first time we met on the *Telemachus*. But I hate myself just as much for caring about someone who could do what he did, for being friends with a traitor." He grabbed up the shin piece and wire pad, and set about scouring the enameled paint again. "I'll be fine, captain. It's just going to be a long time before I'm over it."

Erik rose and watched the man work at the armor, wishing he could have done more to alleviate the feelings of guilt and betrayal. "You know, once that armor is scraped clean it would look good with a symbol on the chest plate. Perhaps the bow and arrow, from the banner of the *Telemachus*."

Tom's hands stopped, and he nodded after a few seconds. "Thank you, captain. That's a great idea."

ELEVEN

"A month without more bombings," Janet blurted out as Nat entered the cabin. "Why stop when the security forces were nowhere near finding out who was behind it all?"

Shrugging out of her dirty jumpsuit, Nat could only shake her head. "Perhaps they achieved whatever goal they had? Or maybe the security forces did track them down, but kept it quiet for some reason."

"I can't see that happening. There are still riots with protesters calling for stronger measures to protect their cities from the threat of bombs. The prime minister and his cabinet would've been shouting it from the rooftops if they'd found whoever was behind it."

"It's all way above my pay grade, Janet. They tell me to fix a part of the ship, and I do it. I'll leave the bigger picture to the people getting larger piles of credits." Nat entered the small washroom and stepped into the shower, hearing her roommate call out from the other room.

"That's not the mindset you need to have. We all have to take an interest, or people like this bomber will never be deterred from creating more chaos and terror."

Rinsing herself off, Nat pulled a towel from the rack and began to wipe away the water that hadn't been blown away by the short air blast at the end of her shower. "There's too much bad shit going on right now. If I spent all my time worrying about each thing, I'd have no time for work or sleep."

Janet's head appeared around the edge of the doorway, a frown on her face. "So you trust people like Fleet Admiral Holgerson to handle everything instead? That idiot has done nothing since he came aboard but slow everything down."

Chuckling at the memory of the shuttle pilot wiping a bit of dirt from the wing, she tossed the towel back into the rack where it would be dried and freshened. "What's he been up to on the bridge now?"

"He has the captain enforcing a cleanliness check every hour. No dust allowed on consoles, fingerprints have to be wiped from screens before the inspection, and if you show up with the slightest bit of grease on a uniform cuff they'll add a note to your file. How is a frigate supposed to operate like that?"

"Oh, I'm sure it's easy when you have nothing to do but orbital patrols." Nat pulled on loose cotton pants and shirt, sighing with pleasure at the soft feel of the fabric on her skin. Returning to the main room, she flopped onto her bunk. "I've heard rumors that when he was a captain it was seen as a punishment to have to serve on his ship. I guess now we know why."

"I swear, Nat, I get half the work done that I used to. There were twelve requests in the communications queue today, resupply shipments and troop movements that are necessary to complete, and they made me stop for five minutes to clean off the display because the admiral saw a few fingerprint smudges."

"He came through Engineering a few days after coming on board. Tried to pull the same thing down there, and the Chief gave him an earful about how a clean engine room is one that never gets used. Hasn't been back since."

Janet climbed into her bunk above, sighing heavily. "I wish the captain would do the same thing. But he knows too well that his career could be ruined with a snap of the admiral's fingers."

"Let's just hope he loosens up once we're in action against those Syndicate ships." Nat closed her eyes, not wanting to think of the fight that was getting closer every day. "The first of the Syndicate frigates is supposed to be reaching the cruiser pretty soon, from what I've heard."

"Tactical crew on the bridge estimate three days for the first, with the second and third each another day behind." Janet's tone had turned somber at the change in subject. "Do you really think arming the Guild freighters is going to help us against that thing?"

"It can't hurt to have a little extra firepower. Dex seems to feel confident that they'll be able to contribute enough to change the odds."

"How's your sister doing? Still on Luna?"

"Yeah, and I've given up trying to convince her to leave. I think she's going to stay there through whatever happens, and work as hard as she can to fight against the Syndicate until the end." Nat rubbed at an eye that grew watery as she spoke. "I should give her a call and check in."

"I need to do the same with my parents," Janet said from above. "They've been talking about moving back into New York City now that it seems the bomb threat is gone."

Putting on earbuds, Nat pulled up the video chat function on her tablet and initiated a connection with Luna. Routing through to her sister, she waited as the screen showed that it was attempting to connect. She was about to end the call when the screen changed to show Dexterity, a comfortable view of home behind her.

"Wow! I think this is the first time I've called in months and not found you in the office."

"Hey, Nat. Meyers sent me home and told me to take a day off. He's been forcing time off on everyone, said we've been working too hard."

"That is a smart man. You've been pushing harder than you need to, sis."

Smiling, Dex held up a finger to point at the camera and then herself. "Pot, meet kettle." They laughed. "How are things going on the *Waterloo*? Still making preparations to head out and meet the cruiser?"

"Every day, and there always seems to be more to do than time to do it in. The ship is still bursting at the seams, but they keep stuffing more people and supplies in. As long as they don't force another roommate on me and Janet, I'll put up with it."

"Is there any kind of ETA on leaving orbit? You know the Syndicate cruiser is only a few weeks from reaching Mars."

Nat frowned, her eyebrows drawing in. "I know, it's one of the things everyone is talking about lately. I don't think many people are happy that we haven't already left orbit to try and defend the joint scientific colony there."

Dexterity looked around the view, as if ensuring that no one was around in Nat's room. "Don't spread it around, but I've heard rumors that the Coalition Parliament decided to let the Syndicate have Mars. Not worth the effort, I think was what it boiled down to."

"What? Are you serious?"

"Unfortunately, yes. President Meyers tried to protest the decision, but they didn't care to hear his input."

Nat couldn't believe that the Navy would agree to leave several hundred people undefended so callously. "Maybe they'll pass it by and leave them be if they see the Coalition forces remaining around Earth?"

"Fingers crossed."

"What about that special project you've been working on? You're always so mysterious about it, but is it coming along?"

Dexterity grimaced and shrugged. "It's not going as smoothly as I'd hoped. I don't think we're going to have the results we wanted before the cruiser arrives, but it might still come in handy down the line. I wish I could tell you all about it, but it's being kept under wraps so tightly that I'm the only person the president is allowing to work on it."

"Give mom a call while you're relaxing at home, okay? She's always asking me about you."

“Already did, Nat. It was the first thing I did when I left the Guild offices.”

“And *that* is why you’re the better daughter.” With a smile, they ended the call and Nat put the tablet away. She could hear Janet speaking softly above her, still connected with her parents. Zipping into the bed, she dropped into a restless sleep with dreams of black-armored soldiers and red dust.

A few days later, Nat was working in the docking bay again. It seemed as if there were tasks drawing her back to the vast area that filled half a dozen decks at the aft of the frigate several times each week. The admiral’s shuttle still sat in the middle of the open floor, the traffic of people and carts flowing around it like a trail of ants diverting around an obstacle placed in their path.

Stepping into the bay control room, she saluted Lieutenant Simon. The officer looked almost exactly as harried and stressed as always, and she was beginning to wonder if he had any other mode. “Lieutenant, Chief said you need assistance getting a couple of docking cranes rerouted?”

“Ah, Nat. Welcome back to my little kingdom.” He set down his ever-present coffee cup, and stepped out onto the catwalk with her to gesture high above. “The admiral has decided that each frigate is going to carry half a squadron of fighters. Which means we have to clear space on the highest racks. Unfortunately, that also means moving a couple of cranes so they can reach the shuttles and old personnel carriers that have been stored up there for far too long."

She examined the space above, and the placement of the mounts where cranes could be moved into position as needed. "Okay, we can make that happen. If you can spare a couple people, we should have the cranes moved into place and connected in a few hours." Her eyes traveled across the various small shuttles. "Where are you going to put the shuttles that get moved to make room for the fighters?"

The lieutenant sighed heavily, shaking his head. "They're being transferred to Luna, for some project in the shipyards there. It'll leave us with only two armored personnel shuttles, but the admiral gets what the admiral wants."

"We live to serve," Nat replied with a grin.

She set to work on getting cranes moved into place to easily stow and retrieve the fighters, spending several hours on the work to ensure that everything was connected and working to her satisfaction. The two docking bay crewmen working with her gossiped throughout, trotting out rumors and theories about every little thing until she wanted to scream with the frustration of the shifting viewpoints.

Finally pronouncing the work completed to her satisfaction, she dismissed the men in time to watch a large shuttle pass through the ion barrier that separated the vacuum of space from the pressurized interior. It landed mere feet from the pristine shuttle that belonged to the Fleet Admiral, needing all the available space to fit within the confines of the docking bay.

Two Marine squads emerged from the shuttle, their polished cobalt Coalition armor reflecting the lights of the docking bay as they marched in a tight formation. She knew the arrival of more Marines would lead to more work as they stuffed additional people into quarters and training rooms that were already overtaxed and straining the limits of the systems in place.

Behind the Marines, eight men and women strolled down the ramp. Their darker blue uniforms singled them out as the pilots who would fly the half dozen Kestrel class fighters that would soon be loaded above her. She was several decks above the floor of the bay, but could tell that the pilots were shorter than average, selected for their ability to comfortably operate within the tight confines of the fighter cockpits.

One of the admiral's aides rushed into the bay to greet the pilots, his words lost in the distance. She watched them being escorted out of the docking bay, one of the men looking up at the two Kestrels stored high above and then swiveling his head to look at where she leaned against the railing. Nat raised a hand, and her lips quirked as the pilot returned the half-hearted wave before exiting to the corridors beyond.

She was tempted to stay and watch as the additional four fighters were brought on board the *Waterloo* and loaded into racks, but there was a long list of work waiting and she'd procrastinated too long already. With a sigh, she pulled out her tablet to mark the docking bay job complete and brought up details for the next one.

Twelve

The frigate was slowing, several hours away from intercepting the *Indomitable.* Davis stood in front of his assault soldiers as they watched the ship on a magnified view. Each member of the squad was kitted out with the black armor, but also had small packs strapped to their backs.

"This is a perfect opportunity to test your skills," the lieutenant said, raising a hand to point at the frigate on the display. "For this exercise, we are going to traverse the distance to our target with compressed air jets. The trip should take forty five minutes. You will not be tethered to a ship, or to each other. If you make a mistake out there, no one will be there to save you."

He looked around at each soldier, ensuring that they understood the magnitude of the situation. "Once we have intercepted the frigate, we will infiltrate. The Marines on board know this is an exercise. However, aside from the captain and his XO, the crew and passengers have *not* been notified. This will add an element of reality to the boarding. Any questions so far? Lopez?"

"Sir, if the crew doesn't know we're coming, doesn't that risk someone resisting with live fire weapons?"

Davis smiled and nodded. "Yes, it does. So don't get shot." The rest of the troops laughed nervously.

He motioned to Anders, and the sergeant stepped forward. "Alright, Ghost Squad. Our target for this mission is the bridge of the frigate. Mission objective is to take control of the ship, fallback objective is disabling it."

Anders turned and manipulated the image of the frigate until they were looking at a highly magnified view of the top hull. He circled an area with a finger. "This is our target landing zone, and this maintenance airlock is our projected entry point. If you land outside the target zone, you'll hustle to join the rest of us before boarding the frigate. Those of you still outside the ship when we enter that airlock are stuck on the hull until the exercise is complete."

With a press of a button, the display changed to show a wireframe view of the frigate deck plans. "Our entry point is only two hundred meters from the bridge. This is the same layout we ran simulations on the last four days, so you should all be familiar with it." Anders turned and pointed at four of the soldiers. "You're Group One, with the lieutenant. The rest of you are Group Two, with me."

Davis stepped forward again. "We're not using insertion pods for this exercise, but everything else will be the same procedure. Report to the torpedo chambers for an assisted exit from *Indomitable*." The assault squad broke into their two groups, and were chatting quietly with each other as they left the briefing room. Anders and Davis saluted each other before following their respective group.

Being fired from a torpedo tube was no big deal when encased in a specialized insertion pod. Doing it outside of the pod was unpleasant at the best of times. Davis watched as the four soldiers were loaded in and ejected from the ship, and then stepped forward for his turn. The weapons tech who helped him slide into the tube had a wide grin, shaking his head at the fact that anyone would want to do something so crazy.

Once the hatch was closed and locked down behind him, Davis was trapped in a small space with no light at all. If not for training that had seen him endure similar conditions for hours at a time, he knew he would have felt a great deal of claustrophobia. He took deep, even breaths as he waited.

A loud hiss signaled the tube firing, and he felt the pad he was lying on shoot forward. All the blood in his body rushed toward his hands and feet, leaving him light-headed and tingling. When he exited the tube at the bow of the cruiser, he was traveling more than two thousand kilometers per hour on top of the cruiser's speed. That momentum carried him into the vast gulf of space, and he turned his helmet to look at the barely visible frigate that was their target.

His HUD showed that all of the assault squad had left the tubes on target. Their projected paths intersected with the location the frigate should inhabit at the time of intercept. It made him proud to see that every member of his team was calm and relaxed. Even the newest members of the team had received enough training outside the cruiser to be comfortable in open space.

Five minutes before intercept, he gave the order to start firing air jets from their packs. Used correctly, the small puffs of air would push each soldier into the target area so they could quickly regroup and enter the ship. At twenty seconds, he started a visual countdown in their HUDs and everyone used the air packs to slow their momentum.

Davis flipped his body expertly a second before impact with the hull, and his magnetic boots locked onto the steel plating at the first contact. He checked his HUD and saw that almost every member of the team had managed to land in the target area, with only one a few meters outside of it. They had all earned a commendation for that show of skill.

Anders and a few of the squad were already at the airlock when he arrived, with one soldier clipping on to exposed wiring. Within moments, the airlock hissed open and the team was able to enter the ship. In less than a minute after impact on the ship, the entire assault team was through the airlock and unstrapping the compressed air packs.

Using hand signals, Davis divided the groups and motioned for Anders to take point. Group Two raised their stun pistols to a resting position as they stepped into the corridor. The soldiers moved quickly to the junction where another corridor crossed theirs, and then checked around the corners. Seeing no one, they waved for Group One to cross. One then kept watch as the other half of the team joined them.

Once on the other side of the junction, Davis had his team take the point and lead the way deeper into the frigate. There was one more corridor junction ahead, only a few meters from the entry to the ship's bridge. The soldiers were steps away when two crew members turned into their corridor, talking to each other. Group One stiffened and raised their weapons, and two stun bolts were fired even as one of the frigate crew looked up in astonishment to see the menacing assault squad.

Davis had the two unconscious people dragged to the side of the corridor, making sure they were treated carefully and left in a comfortable position. Meanwhile, Group Two moved forward and checked the corridor junction to ensure they weren't surprised by other wandering crew. It had been great luck to only see two crew members on a ship overstuffed with extra people for the *Indomitable.*

The assault squad crossed the junction and huddled around the controls to enter the bridge. Davis or Anders could have easily entered their override codes, but that wouldn't be an option if this were a Coalition frigate. The soldier carrying the tech kit stepped up and started to pull off a panel next to the small pad. While he stripped wires and connected his device, the rest of the team kept their eyes behind on the nearby junction point.

It took only ten seconds to bypass the panel security, and the door could be opened with a touch of a button. Anders motioned to proceed, and as soon as the doors hissed open his team hurried into the bridge. A Marine was standing guard just inside the door, and was disabled silently with a stun bolt. He slumped down on the floor as the rest of the squad entered and closed the door behind them.

The bridge was a hive of activity, with eighteen stations fully staffed and engaged. Junior officers were walking between consoles, and one turned to call something up to the command deck. His eyes caught the movement of the assault squad, and his mouth opened in shock when he saw ten weapons pointed at him. A stun bolt hit high in his shoulder just as he squawked a surprised cry.

Anders took Group Two into the bridge, the five soldiers motioning for the crew to step away from their stations and get to the floor. A few started to resist, but once two more people had been knocked out with stun bolts the others accepted defeat and did as ordered.

Davis led his group up the stairs to the command deck. A flechette round passed by his head, his suit's sensor system telling him it had been a soft tipped training round. He stormed up the remaining stairs and pointed his weapon at the Marine by the door. The woman nodded, lowered her weapon, and stepped back to signify that she knew he would have taken her down with a quick shot.

The officers sitting at the row of consoles at the back wall looked at the Marine with stunned shock. They'd clearly not been warned of the training exercise. Davis chuckled at the thoughts he knew had to be whirling through their heads. The captain and a commander stood by the deck railing, both with hands held at their sides.

Group One filled the command deck, each soldier positioned to cover every person in the small area. The captain smiled, and stepped forward. "Don't worry, these soldiers are with us. This is the Ghost Squad that Admiral Yumata has been so proud of for the last few years. It's good to see you in action and find his admiration well placed."

Lieutenant Davis holstered his weapon, and reached up to remove the imposing helmet his team wore. Tucking it under an arm, he snapped a salute to the senior officers on the command deck. "Captain, thank you for letting my team run this training exercise on your ship. I'm pleased to say that my assault squad has performed admirably. It took us only seven minutes and forty-two seconds from breach to control of the bridge."

"Hm. Admirable for your team, but less for my own security forces." The captain raised an eyebrow at the Marine standing at the door. "I think we may need to run more drills of our own on how to prevent boarding from hostile forces."

Down below, Anders had removed his own helmet and was helping crew members to their feet. The three people who had been stunned with low voltage rounds were already coming around, helped into chairs. As the captain got on the ship-wide intercom to announce the training exercise, the sergeant smirked up at Davis and gave a thumbs up.

Ghost Squad spent the rest of their time on the frigate running through how they entered. The Marine squads were assembled to hear the progress, and view video feeds from the squad's helmet cams. By the time they were docked with *Indomitable* and Davis was leading his team back to their home, he felt confident that the frigate would not be surprised by such an invasion again.

THIRTEEN

When the first frigate rendezvoused with the *Indomitable*, Tuya watched from behind the mesh screen of a service tunnel vent as new crew members and Marines were brought into the ship. She examined every nuance of the process, watching as the cruiser's Marines scanned identity cards to enter the details of each person into the systems. Two hundred crew members and three squads of Marines came off the frigate, a number that must have had them living cheek to cheek during the trip out from Earth. Especially since several dozen cargo pods and hundreds of multi-sized containers were also offloaded to one of the *Indomitable*'s cargo bays. The numbers reassured her, and reinforced her belief that in such a crush a single person could easily be lost. Anyone who didn't remember seeing her on a frigate would just assume that she'd been in a separate area with dozens of others they would not recognize.

The second frigate arrived a little more than a day later, mere hours after the offloading of the first had completed. Tuya was ready, wearing her purloined engineering jumpsuit and carrying an identity card that she had found among the many unused storage rooms. It took half a day to find an exploit that allowed her into the security systems. After that it took a few hours of trial and error to alter the card to show her picture and a fake name when scanned.

As the first wave of new crew members streamed from the airlock chamber, she opened the mesh screen and squeezed through to join the throng. Her luck held, and no one noticed her appear from somewhere other than the airlock itself, one man just giving her a bored look as she bumped against him to join the line.

Approaching the squad of Marines that were checking ID cards and keeping a watchful eye on the nearest newcomers, she could feel sweat trickling between her shoulder blades. Her nerves were being stretched to their limit, and she knew that if the identity card she carried was recognized as fake then she would be in for a difficult escape. She had to fight her body to keep from betraying her nervousness by licking her lips constantly, or rubbing at the beads of sweat on her brow. Instead, she kept her eyes forward and down, shuffling slowly toward the Marines as the line moved steadily.

"ID," a Marine finally said to her as she reached the front of the line. She held the card out to be scanned by a small handheld device, and waited as seconds that felt like years ticked by. She could see nothing of the man's expression behind his lowered faceplate, and his posture had not changed at all in the time she had been standing in the line.

"Smith, Delta." He announced the words as her faked identification came up on the screen, then waved her forward to keep the line moving. She struggled to keep a victorious smile from her lips as she kept walking, approaching a group of crew carrying tablets and checking the names that appeared there from the ID scans. A mid-ranked officer stood at the back of the group, a blue haze visible over his right eye from an implanted holo display. Tuya was surprised to see the technology aboard the military ship, since the price had always been exorbitant and out of reach to all but the wealthiest civilians of either superpower.

A woman looked up from her tablet and waved Tuya over. "Delta Smith, engineering and maintenance crew member?"

"Yes, that's me." She tried to smile, but the woman had already looked down and was flipping through screens on the tablet.

"We have openings in Docking Bay Three, so you'll be assigned there. Have you worked on shuttles before?"

"I have a small amount of experience with them," Tuya lied.

"I'll make a note to have you paired with an experienced partner." The woman pulled a small scanner from a holster at her waist, and motioned for Tuya to hold up her ID card so she could scan it. "Your cabin and work assignments are transferred. Use the card at any terminal throughout the ship to get directions."

The woman turned to process the next person, and Tuya stepped away to join the line of others who had already received assignments and were trying to find their new billets. She found an unused terminal several hundred feet down the corridor, and held her ID card over the screen for a second. The display changed to show her face, name, and details of her assigned living and work quarters. Pressing the cabin number, she was surprised to find that it was only a few corridors away from the cabin she had spent the day in after stealing the jumpsuit.

She set off with confident steps, knowing the best route to reach her destination after more than two months of sneaking around the cruiser. After several turns and descending four decks, she stopped at a terminal to pull directions again, thinking that it would make her appear more normal. None of the crew or Marines coming off the frigates would have an idea of the configuration of this first cruiser built by either government. Just in case her records were ever checked, she didn't want to seem too knowledgeable about something like that.

It took half an hour to reach her cabin, and she felt her steps growing lighter as she passed several people and received nothing more than friendly nods in return. With the influx of new people, everyone had lost their suspicion of unrecognized faces. A wide grin spread across her face as she approached the assigned cabin, and waved her card over the sensor by the door.

Entering the cabin, she was greeted by the same arrangement as any other cabin she had been in on the cruiser. There was a tablet waiting on the small table between the chairs of the sitting area. She approached and the screen lit up. *Welcome, Delta Smith* she could see as she grabbed it up. The tablet gathered her biometric data to mark her as the owner, and she felt gratified that she had dumped her "borrowed" device before joining the line of new crew members.

"Hello," a voice called, and she turned to see a woman reclining on one of the bunks. Late thirties, short cut blonde hair, and blue eyes that seemed more curious that Tuya liked. "I guess you're my roommate. I'm Mabel Harris."

"Delta Smith. What department are you in?"

"I am privileged to be one of the finest barmaids in the fleet," the woman replied with a sardonic grin. "But I guess they don't call us that anymore, thankfully. I'm assigned to work as hostess and bartender at some hole in the wall place two decks up."

Tuya raised her eyebrows in surprise. "I thought that kind of thing was done by the ship's AI. No offense."

"None taken, I assure you. Apparently, the Military Committee decided that crew members serving on an elite ship like our new home the *Indomitable* should be graced with better comforts than those usually afforded to them."

"In other words, the officers need to be pampered."

The blonde woman grinned wider. "Got it in one. I think I'm gonna like you, Delta Smith. What's your posting?"

"Bay Three, sounds like I'll be a shuttle mechanic."

"Ah, keeping the oil fresh and the gas topped up in case an officer feels like going out for a drive. Sounds fun."

Tuya furrowed her brows as she tried to keep up with the old-fashioned terms. "You have a thing for history, don't you?"

"Yep, sure do. I actually spent three years of my life studying Earth's history, with a focus on the late nineteenth and early twentieth centuries."

"So you're an historian, and ended up working in a bar on a military warship?" Tuya walked over to sit on the bunk opposite the woman. "How did something like that happen?"

"My parents had crushing debts, my scholarship was canceled before I graduated with my degree, and joining the Navy was my best option for getting a paycheck. Plus, they'll pay for my last year of college if I serve for at least six years. I'm in my fourth." She shrugged with her elbows, hands trapped under her head on the pillow. "The recruiter promised my training would be put to great use. Which apparently meant learning how to mix old cocktails behind a bar in the officer's club of a handful of bases before they plucked me up, put me on a frigate, and I ended up here."

"Wow, that's a harsh reality check." Tuya chuckled along with the other woman. "I guess you get to know all of the officers, though, seeing them in the clubs and talking to them as you mix drinks."

"Oh yes, it's a glamorous position. I have been hit on and propositioned by every single rank it's possible to achieve in the Syndicate military. Both sexes of each rank, too, which makes it even more special."

Tuya relaxed back onto the softness of the bunk, smiling secretively as she thought of ways to use her new roommate. "Well, don't take offence if I wait a while before I hit on you. Maybe I'll sneak into the fancy officer's bar one night and give it a shot."

Mabel turned her head to look across with glinting eyes. "You'll be my special guest, any time you want to get an old-fashioned drink. Just don't be surprised if I accept your proposition to return to your quarters." She winked, and both women burst into laughter. "I definitely like you, Delta Smith. I'm glad you got assigned to my cabin."

Tuya reported for her first shift in the shuttle bay the next morning, still getting used to being able to walk openly along the *Indomitable*'s corridors without having to keep her eyes open for places to duck into and hide. The third frigate was spilling even more people into the increasingly busy hallways as she reported for duty, with three more on the way to add to the numbers of crew and Marines on board.

Entering Docking Bay Three, called the shuttle bay since that was all that the smaller bay held, she found a handful of other crew milling around. She found the man she had been partnered with, a crusty and gray old veteran that reminded her of Fynn, and greeted him with an outstretched hand.

"Delta Smith. I guess you'll be my partner in here."

The man eyed her hand for a moment before shaking it, looking her up and down. "How much experience do you have with shuttle maintenance?"

"Little enough that I'm sure I'll be bugging you with questions a lot more than you'd like," she replied with a slight smile.

He frowned at her and sighed heavily. "Twenty years with the Navy, and this is what I end up with. Training some young newbie." He shook his head in disgust and turned away as an officer in a sharply pressed uniform arrived.

“Welcome to Bay Three,” the man said, his single red rank slash marking him as an ensign. His youthful looks told her that he was probably not long from the academy. “I’m looking forward to getting to know each of you in the days to come. We’re on a grand mission, and I’m sure you’re all as proud to serve on the *Indomitable* as I am. Let’s keep our standards high, and be ready for anything in the weeks to come.”

Turning to gesture around the space that occupied three decks and was half the size of a frigate’s single docking bay, the ensign continued. “As you can see, most of our charges are the assault shuttles that Marines will use against enemy frigates, or to land on colonies or Earth. It is imperative that we keep these shuttles in top condition, because the slightest malfunction could lead to disaster for our brave men and women.

“Now, you have all been assigned partners and allocated a shuttle to work on for today. Get to know the machines you will spending at least the next six months with, and don’t hesitate to ask questions. I’ll be by to meet each of you individually throughout the day.”

Dismissed, Tuya and her grumbling partner approached one of the black shuttles. It was sleek and deadly looking, with short stabilizing wings at the rear that could be extended for atmospheric flight. As her partner showed her how to remove the engine casing and began pointing out the vital parts of that needed to be checked and maintained on a regular basis, she couldn’t help but let a wicked grin spread across her face. With a bit of luck and some hard work, she could make sure the Syndicate war effort suffered a few unexpected setbacks. The opportunity for sabotage was a nice side benefit of her plan to reach her brother.

Tuya found herself enjoying the time she spent in her new role. Mabel proved to be the ideal roommate, since their schedules were different enough to give both of them plenty of time alone in the cabin. When she was around, they shared stories about coworkers and always ended up in laughing fits. On the third night, Tuya accepted an invitation to visit the officer's club two decks up. Mabel had her name added to the guest list, so that her ID card could get her past the door, and mixed drinks like a Moscow Mule and an Old-Fashioned.

"I told you I make old-fashioned drinks," the woman said with a smirk as she set the latter on the bar.

"I didn't think you were being so literal." Taking a hesitant sip, Tuya sampled the drink and then looked up with a smile. "If they all taste as good as this, I'll even put up with your puns."

She spent an hour in the club, looking at the officers who shared the bar and those who had chosen to sit at tables. The variety of rank stripes across the men and women made her think of Davis, the officer who'd been aboard the *Vagabond.* Her hand tightened dangerously around the glass, and she started looking more closely at the officers. Finding the man who had pretended to be their friend, only to have them taken prisoner and spend most of a night beating on her to try and get the freighter's cargo bay unsealed, would be worth having to go into hiding again.

As she was thanking Mabel for the drinks and preparing to leave, the doors slid open to allow entry for a large man who took up most of the doorway as he passed into the room. She recognized Commander Guildersen from when he boarded her old ship with a couple of Marines, ostensibly to greet them. Tuya kept her face turned away from him as he passed, watching him from the corner of narrow eyes.

"Ugh," Mabel groaned. "Guildersen. I was warned about him by the day shift bartender. Apparently, the man will only drink the cheapest swill, and waters it down so much the alcohol practically disappears." She glared at the wide back of the man as he waddled to the back of the room. "A little too free with the hands, too."

"Better you than me," Tuya grumbled. "I'd snap his fat fingers if he tried to touch me."

Mabel laughed, reaching across to tap her on the arm. "I bet you would, too. Then I'd have to go down to the brig to visit you for the rest of my tour."

Tuya was quick to leave as her roommate went to take the commander's order, not wanting to risk being recognized. It had been a fruitful evening for her, having flirted with a few young officers who might prove to be susceptible to her sparse charms, enough to be used in her plans. She would wait a few days and ask Mabel to get her into the officers' club again.

Her work in the shuttle bay was enjoyable for different reasons. The old maintenance crewman she was paired with, Will something-or-other that she couldn't be bothered to remember, continued treating her like a nuisance sent to punish him. And she happily embraced the role, making him show her how to do things over and over until he exploded in anger. When that happened, she started shouting back with a surge of joy as she finally had a chance to release some of the stress, anger, and frustration that had been building up for months. She was always left breathless by the time the man gave up in disgust and stalked away, but the relief she felt gave her a smile that had made others in the shuttle bay look at her askance more than a few times.

The ensign in charge of Docking Bay Three had tried to bring her and Will together to have them hash out their differences, telling them that the shouting matches were causing disruptions in the work. That had not gone well for anyone but Tuya, as she got in the faces of both men and accused them of treating her like a lost little lamb, a young woman who had no place in their greasy men's world of shuttle maintenance. She didn't believe a word of it, but both men had wild looks as they rushed to deny any such feelings about her. The meeting ended with Will promising to be less overbearing, and Tuya promising to take his criticisms less personally. She knew that neither of them really meant it.

Outside of work, she spent hours walking through the corridors of the cruiser completing the map in her head that had been forming since she was trapped on board. There were a few sections of the ship that were barred to those who did not work there, like the bridge and engine rooms, but for the most part she had the run of the ship. She was careful not to pass by the holding cells again, in case her stance was recognized from the times she had been there wearing the old Marine armor.

It took several days, but she worked out a plan for accessing the cells through service tunnels and an empty storage room. She would need to gather a few tools to cut through bulkheads, but she felt confident it could be carried out quietly enough to not be noticed during the three or four hours the process would take.

The biggest hindrance was that she had no idea what the extent of the security would be. Were the Marine guards and cameras obsessively watching the corridors around the holding cells the only obstacle, or would she find stun fields built into the walls that would prevent her plan to cut through them? It was a calculated risk, since encountering such a field would incapacitate her long enough for soldiers to find her and slap restraints on her. She could only hope that the high energy expenditure needed for that level of security had not been deemed worthwhile during construction of the cruiser.

Over a couple of shifts in the shuttle bay, she managed to isolate a metal cutting torch and disassemble it into a handful of pieces small enough to smuggle out at the end of her shifts. She had two parts of it already stashed in the storage room she planned to start her rescue attempt from, and hoped to get the rest out within a week. With the *Indomitable* fast approaching Mars, she knew the activity in the shuttle bay would increase and it would be easier for her to smuggle components out. The last piece, the power source and fuel supply for the cutting tool, was large enough that she would have to choose the perfect moment to slip it out.

Tuya's sixth shift working in the bay began like any other, as she joined the other crew members at their lockers to store items and check on the schedules for the day. Half a dozen assault shuttles were already sitting on the floor of the bay, and she felt her eyes drawn to the dull matte black shuttle that stood out in comparison to the sleek and glossy others. The lines of this shuttle were more angular, and it looked much more deadly and dangerous. She was happy to find that she and her partner were assigned to maintenance duties on a Marine shuttle on the far side of the bay.

Hours passed as she worked, unscrewing and removing panels to reach each part of the engines and shuttle workings. The Syndicate was strict about every shuttle being thoroughly checked before missions, and everyone was harried and stressed with so much to get ready for the ground assault. Tuya glanced around a few times to make sure she was unobserved before loosening some wires and sabotaging a power relay so that it would fail at some point in flight. She chuckled softly at the minor acts of defiance, enjoying her visions of the panic the pilots would experience. She wanted to do more, but knew it was too dangerous when she was so close to being able to effect a rescue of Altan.

Marines filed into the shuttle bay as she worked, and she glared at the squad that stood nearby and seemed to watch her every move. It put her in a bad mood already when Will approached and started to inquire about the progress of the checks.

"Are you still working on that engine, girl? You should've been done half an hour ago!"

Raising a grease-stained middle finger to scratch the cheek facing him, she bent down and shuffled deeper into the compartment to get at a stubborn power coupling that had shifted and needed to be put back into its proper place. "I'll finish when I finish, old man. If you're so fired up about it, why don't you do some actual work and handle this for me?"

"Listen here, you insolent whelp. I finished the same work on the other side of this shuttle, and I've done it faster and better than you can ever hope to. I don't know why they haven't shifted you into a job you can actually handle. Maybe cleaning heads, though even that seems above your comprehension sometimes."

Growling, Tuya jerked the coupling into place and then pulled back to exit the compartment and turn to face Will. She raised a finger to stab at him viciously. "I comprehend just fine that you're a pig of a man who couldn't find shit in a sewer if they showed you pictures beforehand."

"That's it," Will yelled, raising his hands in indignation. "I've had all I'll take out of you. I don't know how you managed to survive the trip out from Earth with that mouth of yours."

"Fantasizing about my mouth now, huh? I always knew you were an old pervert, but now the proof is revealed."

"I'll tell you what I'd do with that mouth. First, I'd pull that foul tongue of yours...." Will broke off suddenly, turning to look behind her with an expression of surprise.

Tuya was about to heckle him for not being able to think of anything to say, and glanced back to see what he was looking at. Behind her were four soldiers in armor that matched the lethal shuttle in color. Two of the soldiers were helmeted, with weapons pointed in her direction. The other two were standing between them with faces exposed, one of them causing her to go white as the blood drained from her face.

FOURTEEN

"You wanted to see me, sir?" Davis stood at attention in front of Commander Guildersen's desk yet again, resisting the temptation to look down and see if his feet were beginning to create imprints in the floor from repeated visits. This time he was in a for a surprise, as the overweight officer greeted him with a smug smile instead of the dire frown that usually preceded one of the dressing downs he still received every few days.

"Well, Lieutenant, the time has finally come to see just how good your assault team really is." He pressed a button on the desk, and a holographic display of Mars and its two moons appeared between them. "The *Indomitable* will be in orbit around Mars in two days. Marine squads will drop to the planet to round up Coalition scientists. Ghost Squad will drop to Deimos to take control of the small colony there. Your orders are to contain all colonists, prevent any damage to the systems, and separate out the Coalition citizens."

"How many colonists on the moon, sir? Can we expect armed resistance?"

"It's a small outpost of little more than one hundred people, mostly serving as a supply point for the scientific missions on the planet itself. Keeps the Guild's precious freighters from having to enter the thin atmosphere in their junk heaps." A wry twist of the officer's mouth showed his disdain for the independent ships. "As to armed resistance, there may be a few stun weapons on the colony. Our latest reports show two security officers, and that is the extent of their protection."

"Very good, Commander. Once we have the Coalition people singled out, what are our orders?"

Guildersen looked him over with slitted eyes. "What do you think your orders will be, Lieutenant?"

Davis knew this was some kind of test, a way for the cruiser's first officer to assert his dominance once again over the special group that the admiral continued to show favor towards. If he answered correctly, his words would be met with scoffs and sarcastic congratulations. If he answered wrong, he had no doubt it would be added to the litany of his faults in each succeeding lecture. "Am I to eliminate them as possible threats, sir?"

"Very good, Lieutenant. You really are one of the best and brightest in our proud Navy." The sneering good humor was nothing less than expected. Guildersen moved a hand to zoom the display to show the misshapen lump of Deimos, twisting the picture so that the colony structures were visible at the top. There were a handful of large blocky buildings, only a few feet of them sticking out above the surface of the moon to expose solar panel arrays that provided a large chunk of the power needed within. One of the buildings was limned in red.

"This is the warehouse and docking platform facility. The colonists will expect you to make your entry there." With a touch of a fat finger, another building started to flash in red. "Instead, I want you to infiltrate this building, medical and hydroponics. Our source within the colony has identified a weakness in the construction of the outer wall that you can exploit."

"Sir, if we enter there, the vacuum will destroy the colony's ability to sustain itself. They will be dependent on shipments of food until the hydroponics can be repaired and replenished."

"That suits us just fine, Lieutenant. My recommendation to the admiral has been to keep all colonies dependent upon the home world for their survival, to prevent this independent operations nonsense in the future. It leads to nothing but trouble."

"Yes, sir." Davis kept his eyes above the Commander's head, jaw clenched tightly as he fought an urge to voice his own opinions on why such a policy would cause more troubles in the future than independent operations ever could. He listened to the rest of the operational briefing and limited himself to short replies where necessary, escaping the room as soon as he was dismissed.

"But sir, once we breach that wall the entire building will be exposed to vacuum. Won't that kill anyone working in there at the time?"

Davis cast his eyes over the squad, feeling a pride that his team could see the same flaws in the plan that he had. "Yes, unfortunately it will. The Commander's informant on Deimos is supposed to ensure that all Syndicate nationals are kept from working shifts in the building during the proposed entry window."

“The hydroponics are going to be a total loss,” another soldier said, taking advantage of the team policy to voice all thoughts during mission briefings. Davis felt that it kept them more focused, and helped to smooth out any wrinkles that might come up during a mission.

“Again, yes they will.” He paused and looked over the displayed map of the colony buildings. “Would any of you suggest an alternate entry point?”

Anders raised an inquisitive eyebrow at the question, silently asking if his commanding officer was really considering changing the mission parameters. Davis nodded slightly, and turned to one of the soldiers who had raised a hand to speak. He recognized her as Lopez, the youngest member of the squad who had stood out several times in training exercises over the last several months.

“Sir,” the young woman began tentatively. “I know the brief says the docking facility should be avoided because the colonists will expect us there, but couldn’t that be used in our favor?”

“How so, Lopez?”

She rose from her seat and approached the displayed map, manipulating the holographic display to zoom in on the building and surrounding area. “This small door is where the shuttle that transports supplies to and from the Martian surface is stored. It’s a Syndicate-produced model, so we should have the override codes in our systems. If we can get a remote connection, then commands to open the exterior door can be routed through the shuttle. The colonists think that someone is entering from that direction, and divert their attention."

Lopez flipped the view to display the opposite side of the building. "The airlock for repair and maintenance of the solar arrays is here. While the attention of the colonists is on the shuttle hangar, we can get part of the team through the airlock with a quick entry/exit procedure."

"The systems on colonies aren't set up for QE/E," Anders interjected.

"No, sir, but I've run some simulations with forcing it via a tablet hard-wired into the colony systems. We can set that up before starting the shuttle distraction, and then a simple command will force the airlock to cycle open and closed without depressurizing."

Davis looked at the map as he considered the proposal. "The group selected to enter will have to be well clear of the airlock in case it's pressurized and the atmosphere vents."

Lopez nodded enthusiastically. "Yes, sir, at least a couple of dozen meters. We can cover that space quickly if we use suit thrusters to approach and enter the airlock as soon as it's clear. Once inside, the QE/E can cycle the outer door closed and the open the inner door half a second later."

"The pressurized air will definitely rush in at that point," Davis told her. "The team inside will need to be ready to brace themselves until the pressure equalizes."

"Our assault suits can handle that kind of intensity," Anders added hopefully. "We could have a group inside the colony complex within sixty seconds, and the second group could follow just as quickly to assist."

“Thank you, Lopez.” Davis nodded, and the young woman returned to her seat with a smile. “Does anyone here have objections to the new plan, or proposals for alternate entries?” He looked around and saw everyone giving a negative head shake. “Very well, I’ll submit this mission change proposal to the admiral and see if he approves.”

“What are our orders once we get inside, sir?” Anders gave a wry grin as he asked the question, knowing the admiral would approve the change with Davis’s full support behind it.

“Thank you, sergeant. Once we make it inside the colony, we are to gain control of the facility with minimal damage. Command wants the systems fully operational when we leave orbit. We separate the colonists into groups of Syndicate citizens and Coalition citizens.” Davis paused and swept his eyes over the team again as he spoke, judging their reactions to the next part. “Mission briefing says there are one hundred and twelve colonists, latest intel is that forty nine of them are from the Coalition. When we leave Mars, the colony should have sixty three colonists and will be in full Syndicate control.”

There was a slight murmur among the squad members at the news, but no one objected to the order. “The training bay is being configured for the ground assault mission, and I’ll send the support staff our proposed plan changes. First training is at fourteen hundred. I want to run through it at least five or six times today and tomorrow so that we’re fully prepared when the *Indomitable* arrives in orbit around Mars. Dismissed.”

The admiral had been quick to approve the new plan that Davis proposed, a fact that was heavily mentioned in the very next ranting lecture he endured in Guildersen's office. The Commander despised him even more after this demonstration of how much more influence the Lieutenant had.

Ghost Squad ran training scenarios tirelessly as the cruiser approached the red planet, with Davis throwing obstacles of all kinds in their path to prepare them for every eventuality. In the nine training sessions, the assault team managed to infiltrate and secure the colony with minimal damage and no Syndicate casualties seven times. It was a success rate that had the soldiers yelling gleefully as they were dismissed from the last session to enjoy a night off.

"I'm recommending Lopez be promoted to corporal, sir." Anders had found him after the final training session, the joy of success all over his face.

"You'll have my support for that, Sergeant. I have also submitted her name as a candidate for officer school at the academy once we're back at Earth. The ingenuity and skill she's shown over the last few months have truly impressed me."

"She'd make a good Lieutenant, sir. Of course, that means we'll probably have to train some newbie again."

"That's what I have you for, isn't it?" They shared a laugh before making plans for the landing and assault the next day. The *Indomitable* would be in orbit around Mars within fourteen hours, and intersecting the orbit of Deimos an hour after.

"I've already put in a request to have our shuttle prepped and ready before we reach orbit. My plan is to exit the bay early, and use momentum from the cruiser to approach the moon from the opposite direction of the colony."

"Good plan, sir. Unless our intel is incredibly erroneous, they don't have a sensor station beyond the radius of the colony complex. We can land undetected and approach on foot."

"Make sure we have extra oxygen and nitrogen canisters in the shuttle, Sergeant. If we have to reassess our entry based on what we see on the ground, I want to be able to refill our suit supplies."

Saluting, Anders left to ensure that their assault shuttle was loaded with all the gear the team would need, leaving Davis to complete his own preparations for the mission. It would be the first chance for Ghost Squad to show their skills in a live mission, and he was determined to prove that the admiral's faith in him was not misplaced.

The shuttle bay was a hive of activity as the assault team entered and approached their matte black shuttle, looking almost shabby next to the glossy surfaces of the shuttles that would drop Marine squads to the surface of Mars over the next few days. Anders ushered the team onboard and had everyone double check the gear bags, while Davis made a circuit of the shuttle and checked over the hull. He knew their assigned pilot would have already made the same checks, but it set his mind at ease to know that another pair of eyes had been over the shuttle.

Minutes seemed to be draining away, and when he checked his wrist display he saw that there was only half an hour to go before the cruiser attained orbit. His shuttle would depart fifteen minutes later. He was dressed in the same black armor as the rest of his team, minus the helmet which waited inside the shuttle to be slipped over his head at the last minute.

Stopping near the open ramp of the shuttle, he could hear Anders barking orders at the squad as they ran through the lists of necessary tools and weapons for the mission. With a smile, Davis stepped away to watch the activity elsewhere in the shuttle bay.

A single squad of Marines waited near a shuttle on the far side of the bay, ready to board as soon as the shuttle bay crew members working on it gave a green light. He was wondering how soon the squad would be dropping to approach the first scientific team on the surface, when a familiar figure caught his eye. Davis focused on the person in the red jumpsuit, bent over an open engine cowling. There was something about the posture and almost angry movements of the individual that had drawn his attention, and he stepped closer unconsciously as he willed them to turn so he could see a face.

An older man approached the worker, hands waving and mouth moving as he spoke about something that was lost in the cacophony of sounds in the busy shuttle bay. The person pulled their upper body from the open engine panel, turning to respond to the man with obvious indignation.

Davis gasped at the sight of the woman's profile, a satisfied smile spreading across his face.

"Anders," he said after activating the assault suit communications. "Join me in the bay with a couple of our squad, please."

Half a minute later, the sergeant approached with two fully suited squad members following. "What's up, sir? Did we miss something?"

"Follow me, and be ready to use those weapons." Davis strode across the shuttle bay with purpose, barely noticing the Marine squad turning to look at his small group. He stopped twenty feet away from the shuttle, and the older crewman closed his mouth in surprise as he turned to the armed soldiers holding weapons in his direction. His wide eyed expression caused the woman to turn and look, as well, surprise turning into frustration and then anger.

"Hello, Miss Sansar," Davis said with a smile.

FIFTEEN

"Luna Control, this is the freighter *Vagabond*, requesting docking clearance." Mira spoke with the confidence of years in a pilot's chair, though it had been most of a decade since she last went through docking procedures. Erik watched and listened with a small smile, ready to jump in if she forgot some minor part of the normal routine.

"*Vagabond*, Luna Control. Clearance granted, please proceed to docking platform Aldrin 5."

"Thank you, Control. *Vagabond* out." She smoothly shifted their course to approach the appointed landing site, and Erik settled in for the long process of landing and completing a connection to the shipyard. It was the first time in years that his ship had been directed to one of the Aldrin dome platforms, another sign that tensions between the two governments were heating up.

On the approach to Luna, he had seen a fleet of Guild freighters in orbit around the moon, the *Tamerlane* joining them as the eleventh. On the planet, another five were found on docking platforms just outside Aldrin, with shipyard workers swarming over one as the hull was examined and light railguns were added to the ship. His ship made a total of seventeen Guild freighters clustered at Luna, leaving two more still out in the system somewhere. He hoped they were on the way to join the rest, or at least safe wherever they had ended up instead.

The trip to Luna had taken a few days longer than he'd hoped, but they still arrived before the Syndicate cruiser reached Mars. According to the latest course projections, the warship was just days away from arriving at the red planet. Erik had tried to get in touch with Dex as they entered Lunar orbit, but she had been busy with other things according to the Guild representative he spoke with.

Arrangements had then been made for the *Vagabond* to land, and they were moved into a priority position on the shipyard list to have the second heavy railgun installed on the belly of the ship. He grinned every time he entertained fantasies of firing fifty kilogram depleted uranium rounds at the *Indomitable* with guns that had been meant for her.

Air hissed into the ship as the airlock opened and Erik entered the flexible tube to cross into Aldrin's docking complex. The rest of the crew was preparing the freighter for work that would soon begin, and Fynn was adamant about being part of the process. "No one touches my hull without me being there to make sure they don't screw up," he 0said loudly when Erik suggested that he could use a few days off the ship.

The airlock at the other end opened to reveal President Meyers waiting to greet him with an enthusiastic handshake. Dex was standing just behind, her face down as fingers flew across the surface of the tablet she was holding. "It's a pleasure to meet you in person, Captain Frost. The Guild and the Coalition both owe you a very large debt for your warnings." Meyers smiled unctuously, the expression of politicians everywhere working to keep their constituents happy.

“I just wish my warnings could have done something for the people on Interamnia, sir.”

“Yes, that was an absolutely horrible act of violence. I can’t tell you how much that rattled all of us here on Luna, and on Earth. No one thought the Syndicate capable of such a monstrous act.”

“One would’ve hoped it would spur action, not pulling all the Coalition frigates to cluster around the home world.” Erik couldn’t hide his frustration, even in the presence of the leader of his Guild.

Meyers nodded, waving a hand forward to indicate they should walk and talk. “Personally, I share your frustrations on that front. I have been recommending a more aggressive response for months, as Dexterity could tell you. The prime minister has been reluctant to act, however, especially after the terrorist bombings.”

“Which is probably just what the Syndicate wanted.” Erik looked back, trying to catch Dex’s attention but unable to as she continued to work frantically on the tablet. She walked with her head down, and the ease with which she followed their steps told him it was an action she’d grown very accustomed to.

“We don’t yet know that the Syndicate was behind the bombings,” President Meyers cautioned. “Until we have hard proof, accusing them of the attacks will do nothing but cause more tension between the governments.”

“Yeah, wouldn’t want something like several thousand deaths and a destroyed mining colony to stand in the way of holding on to the status quo.”

Meyers chuckled, surprisingly. “Dex was right, you and I will get along very well.” The man dropped his obsequious manner and even seemed to stand straighter as they walked through Aldrin toward the Guildhall. “Let me ask you a question, Erik. How far are you willing to go to protect Luna and Earth from the Syndicate cruiser?”

“As far as I have to, sir. I’d fly a nuclear bomb right into their belly, if I could.”

“Excellent! You’re just the man I want. I’m going to lay out a plan for you and see if you’ll join in.”

Meyers would say no more as they walked, too aware of the other people passing by or standing in doorways and on balconies overlooking the streets. Erik turned back again, and caught a faint smile as Dex’s eyes darted up to meet his for a few seconds. He felt a weight lift from his shoulders that he hadn’t realized was there.

Entering the Guildhall was like arriving at a disaster zone. Twice as many desks had been shoved into the area since his last trip to Luna, and there were dozens of people rushing between them carrying messages and coordinating activities. The noise of it all was almost deafening in the tight space. Erik followed Meyers through to the office at the far end. He could feel the eyes of everyone on him as he passed, sure that they were wondering why he rated such special treatment.

Meyers waved him into a chair, closing the door on the noise of the main room and sitting in the large leather chair behind a narrow glass-topped desk. Dex had followed them in, crossing to sit in a padded chair to thc side of the desk as she continued tapping at the tablet.

"Would you like a drink, captain? I keep a selection of fruit juices on hand, fresh from Earth every day." Erik accepted a glass of cold orange juice, sipping at the tart drink and closing his eyes to enjoy the taste. Most fruits cultivated in the hydroponic farms on the colonies were soil-grown fruits like strawberries, blueberries and raspberries. Tree fruits were rare, and expensive when found.

"Shipyard crew are starting work on the *Vagabond* now, sir," Dex spoke up. "Estimated completion time is sixty-two hours."

"Excellent. We'll have your ship fully armed and ready to go faster than I expected, Erik."

"There was some damage to our bow during the AI incident, so they may have to do some repairs that extend the completion time."

Meyers smiled, leaning back in his chair and steepling his fingers. "I have you set up for a full frame refit and almost entirely new hull plating. The Coalition gave us every credit we asked for, and I asked for enough to give my captains a solid chance of getting through any fight."

Erik was stunned at the news that his ship was about to receive the improvements and upgrades he'd hoped to save up for within a few years. "That's a fast turnaround on such an intensive job. I was told it would take two to three months for a refit like that."

"Normally, yes. We have all the workers concentrating on one ship at a time. They're putting in long hours, with as many extra hands as they can get on the job. It's costing an arm and a leg, but it's worth it if we get the entire fleet ready for battle."

"Speaking of the fleet, sir, I noticed we're two freighters short when we came in. Are they on the way?"

"Been and gone," Meyers said with a tug of the lips. "Part of the plan I wanted to discuss with you. The *Vagabond* is going to be the most heavily armed freighter thanks to those guns you stole from the Syndicate." He raised a hand to forestall protests. "Didn't deliver to the Syndicate, if you like. Either way, you'll be packing enough firepower to be perfect for a job I have in mind. Are you willing to hear me out?"

Erik glanced over at Dex, seeing that she had stopped typing and was paying close attention to the conversation. She nodded faintly, and he took it as encouragement. "I'm in, sir, but I'll need to have my crew agree to it as well before I can sign on. No more accepting jobs without the full details and support of my team."

Meyers grinned and slid a folder across the desk, real paper inside the beige plastic cover. "Read over this, and see what you think."

Erik left the Guildhall late in the evening, stepping into artificial twilight with the dome's lighting lowered to create a day/night pattern. He had spent several hours closeted with the President of the Guild, some of it talking with his crew over an encrypted connection to the control room on the *Vagabond*. The plan was outlined, and each of them enthusiastically agreed to accept a role. Even Fynn, who had grumbled about having to leave the work on the hull for the duration of the conference.

Standing next to a small stretch of real grass on the open square, Erik breathed in the smells of the dome. He still felt angry and frustrated about what had been happening the last few months, but now that he was finally doing something constructive he also felt hopeful and impatient to begin. He kept reminding himself it was only three days of waiting before they could depart and begin their role in Meyers' plan.

"I like this time of day best. It's always so quiet and peaceful." Dex stepped up beside him, looking over the darkened square and the closed shops that surrounded it. Windows above the shops were lit with soft light, and the sounds of music and laughter could be heard from several places. Light and noise came from down a street on the far side of the square, a restaurant entertaining the late crowd.

"Absolutely beautiful," Erik agreed, his eyes on her face. "How are you doing, Dex?"

She turned amber eyes to meet his, a small smile on her lips. "I'm doing better now that I can stop worrying about you for a while. I'm glad to see you again, Erik."

Steeling himself, he wrapped an arm around her shoulders and pulled her close in a hug. Dex laid her head on his shoulder, sliding an arm around his back. "I suppose it's too late to get that drink?" he asked.

"It's never too late. The Houston Eagle is open," she replied, pointing to the lights down the street. They started to stroll along the edge of the square, staying close. Erik could feel a lump in his throat, nerves almost overwhelming him. After four years of being unable to work up the courage, he was finally getting to spend time with Dex outside the Guildhall.

"I always wondered when you were going to ask me," she said, interrupting his thoughts.

"What? Was I that transparent?"

Chuckling, her arm around his back squeezed tightly. "Erik, you had the biggest puppy dog eyes I've ever seen the first time we met. I knew then that you were trying to work up the nerve to ask me out."

"Heh. I guess I tend to wear my emotions on my sleeve. You can't blame a guy for wanting to spend time with a beautiful woman, though. Especially when he discovers she's also smart and has a wonderfully sarcastic sense of humor."

"Keep talking like that, mister, and you might get more than one drink out of this." She reached across to poke him in the side, eliciting a jerk and laugh as she hit a ticklish spot. They split apart as they arrived at the restaurant, grabbing a small table in a corner of the bar where they could talk quietly as they drank.

Erik knew he would be kept busy over the next several days getting ready for when his ship could depart, but for tonight he planned to enjoy this time with Dex. Looking into her shining eyes, and running his fingers through her curly dark hair, he felt more at peace than he had in years.

Her smile made his heart melt every single time. She smiled a lot that night.

SIXTEEN

The shuttle touched down on the rocky surface of the smallest Martian moon, several kilometers outside the known radius of the colony's limited sensor range. Ghost Squad left the shuttle on two small low profile carts. The electric motors that propelled them contained enough charge for the trip to the colony, and were totally silent. The only noise created by their passage was the spiked wheels digging into the rocky surface to keep the vehicle from bouncing into space.

Davis and his squad were practically reclined in the low carts, with seats dropped back to prevent anything from being more than a few feet above the moon's surface. It was the only way they could be sure that the colony's sensors would overlook their presence as they sped toward their targets at twenty kph.

Both carts stopped behind the low crater rim that surrounded the embedded colony buildings. Anders and Group Two angled off to approach the small shuttle bay door, where they would get a remote connection to the supply shuttle. Group One followed Davis to the maintenance airlock, where Lopez immediately set to work on getting her prepped tablet connected to the panel.

"We have connection with the shuttle," Anders reported within half a minute. "Ready to open doors on your signal, lieutenant."

Davis looked to Lopez, receiving a nod several seconds later. "Do it."

As the shuttle bay door began to open with a hiss of exiting air, Davis looked through the airlock windows and saw emergency beacons begin to flash in the warehouse. A handful of people could be seen running toward the storage area where the supply shuttle was kept, and he was happy to see only one stun pistol among them. The other colonists in view were carrying batons or makeshift staves. He wasn't sure what they thought such crude weapons would do against armed Marines.

At his signal, Lopez executed the quick entry/exit procedure she had created. They hurried away from the airlock as it began to open, a violent spray of pressurized atmosphere escaping into space, blowing dust and small rocks from the moon's surface. Within seconds, they were able to approach and scramble into the airlock, where Lopez initiated the second phase. Each of them braced tightly against the walls of the airlock. The outer door began to close at the same moment that the inner door was opening. Air rushed through the small chamber, buffeting each soldier until the outer door was closed.

Group One pushed forward into the colony's warehouse, with Davis at the rear giving commands to the others. He arrayed his group behind various stacks of containers, and then let his assault suit sensor package scan the colonists. Biometric data for every person on Mars and Deimos was kept in Coalition and Syndicate databases, one of the few benefits the shared scientific outposts had provided.

Within half a minute, the colonists in the warehouse were labeled in their HUDs. Those who were Syndicate citizens were shaded green. Coalition citizens were shaded red. As Davis keyed his sensors to continue running the identification algorithm for anyone else they encountered, he told Lopez to lead the group and subdue those marked out.

The young woman's hand moved quickly through non-verbal commands, and the soldiers followed her out of cover. Stun darts were fired simultaneously to take down the three Coalition citizens in the warehouse, and as Davis stepped out the Syndicate colonists were already laying down their weapons and raising their hands in surrender. "We're with the Syndicate Navy," he assured them. "Remain here, and you will not be harmed."

Group Two joined them as the shuttle bay door slid up. Anders ducked through the opening as soon as he could, quickly scanning the room. Once all ten members of the squad were reunited, they did a quick search of the warehouse to verify there were no colonists hiding away.

Davis led the way into the corridor that branched off ahead. He waved Anders left, where the scientific labs and hydroponics were located. Group One followed him right, toward the living and recreational quarters. The first room they encountered looked like a small classroom. It was vacant at the moment, so he waved the group on.

Deimos colonists shared communal rooms, with individual spaces curtained off for a small amount of privacy. The first living space they entered contained a few dozen beds, and more than twenty colonists were gathered together. Davis's armor quickly scanned and tagged them, and without hesitation the assault team began firing stun darts at anyone shaded red. These bolts were powerful enough to leave someone unconscious for as long as half an hour. Even after recovering, the person would suffer from extreme muscle cramping and soreness for a few days.

The only resistance they faced was in the security office. Five men and women had set up a rough barricade in the doorway. When Davis peeked through the piled furniture, a flechette round was fired with bad aim in his direction. Even before he jerked his head back, his sensor suite had identified all but one of the people in the room. Every one of them was shaded in red.

"What should we do, sir?"

"What would you do in my position, Lopez?"

"Well, we only face five hostiles. One confirmed lethal rifle, four confirmed enemy occupants, one person unconfirmed." She processed the view his camera had recorded during the brief look through the barricade. "Drop a stunner, storm the room, identify the final occupant."

"It's your plan, Lopez. Lead the team." Davis smiled inside his helmet, stepping back to watch how Group One would work under the young woman's leadership.

She tossed the stun grenade herself, flinging it accurately into the center of the room. Several of the occupants cried out a second before the room was filled with blinding light and enough noise to set their ears ringing. Four armored soldiers pushed through the makeshift barricade, firing stun darts the moment one of the occupants was visible.

The fifth person in the room, nationality unconfirmed, was surrounded and wisely dropped the flechette rifle they held. Davis stood over them, watching as the person's outline shifted to a red color in his HUD. "Restrain this one. He's the only one who had the guts to fight back, so we'll let him live the longest."

An hour later, the facility was swept clean and they had forty nine Coalition citizens gathered in one room. Anders was sitting on a cargo crate, his weapon loosely aimed at the colonists huddled together in groups. Most of them had dull lifeless expressions, though a few cried or moaned in fear. Twelve of them were children under seventeen.

Davis had managed to get a connection with the *Indomitable*, reporting the success of his mission. Unfortunately, Commander Guildersen had intercepted his call. "You've done what you were instructed, Lieutenant. I'm not sure if you expect me to pat you on the back for doing your job."

"No, sir," Davis said with a clenched jaw. "I merely wished to report the status of our mission, and ask for further orders with regards to the prisoners."

"Not developing a soft spot, are you?"

Davis didn't respond to the jibe, closing his eyes and cursing himself for not isolating the channel to only his comms. The rest of the squad were listening in, and he could see from their postures that they were taking offense at the way their lieutenant was being treated.

"As I told you before, lieutenant, eliminate the Coalition presence on Deimos. Our Marine squads are already doing the same on Mars. There was one incident with a shuttle losing power during descent and crash landing, but the other squads are proceeding smoothly."

"Yes, sir. My team will wrap up the mission and then return to the ship."

"Wait," Guildersen said just as Davis was about to end the connection. "I've had an idea of how we can use those colonists, after all. Give me five minutes, Lieutenant Davis, and you'll have your orders for cleaning up the trash."

Davis endured the crackling sound of the dead connection for a second before his suit computer shut it down. There had been a tone in Guildersen's voice that he hadn't liked. It was the same tone he'd heard too often when the commander relished in listing every failing of himself or his team. He was almost certain that whatever plan was being worked up, he wouldn't enjoy executing it.

Seventeen

Nat was sitting in the rec room, surrounded by dozens of other off-duty crew, watching the news reports. The Syndicate cruiser had arrived at Mars a week earlier, and information had been slowly trickling out ever since. For days as the *Indomitable* approached, a flurry of messages had gone out from colonists and scientists pleading for help or extraction. The prime minister had been roasted by the media, as everyone asked why more was not being done to protect Coalition citizens on Mars and Deimos. When they went silent, it had been an eerie time of increasing tension as Earth waited to find out what had happened.

The first reports came three days later, a Syndicate broadcast of a haughty older man with Asiatic features standing on the bridge of the warship in a crisp black uniform heavy with badges, metals and rank stripes. "I am Admiral Yumata of the Syndicate cruiser *Indomitable,* currently orbiting Mars. Our people have suffered for too long under harsh restrictions imposed upon us by the Coalition. Constraints that have kept our economy in a near constant state of recession.

"This ship was constructed to allow our people to reclaim their freedom, to grow and prosper as they wish. To that end, I am formally announcing that the Syndicate has taken control of the five remaining asteroid mining colonies; Vesta, Hygeia, Cybele, Davida, and Ceres. The incident on Interamnia was the result of continued resistance to our destined rule, an example to show we will brook no defiance.

"Over the last few days, our Marines have landed on the planet below and on the Deimos colony. In a daring raid, our advanced assault squad made entry to the colony and was successful in containing all citizens and minimizing any damage to the facilities. All Coalition citizens have been eliminated, and the Syndicate is in full control of Mars and the surrounding area going forward.

"I send this message now to warn the people of Luna that you are our next stop. If you are a citizen of the Syndicate, please enter Armstrong dome and do not leave. If you know of Coalition citizens in the dome, do everything in your power to remove them to Aldrin. The Marines based on Armstrong will be performing sweeps to assist with this effort.

"To the citizens of the Coalition, I have only one thing to say. Your time is at an end."

The screen went black for half a minute before the interrupted newscasts returned, the hosts and reporters all struck into stunned silence. Nat had been watching at the moment of the broadcast, feeling the same numbness and shock. When the people around her finally started to voice their anger and concern, she left the rec room to return to her cabin. She had known a few people stationed at the colony on Deimos, faces that she would never see again and people who would no longer trade occasional messages with her.

The news only got worse the next day, as confirmation of the takeover was sent to the media outlets. Black-suited soldiers holding weapons stood to either side of the last surviving Coalition citizen in the colony on Deimos, the man kneeling and weeping as guns were held to his head and he was forced to read a statement that listed the names of everyone killed in the colony. He read forty-eight names, his voice halting and so broken by the sobs that racked his body that names often had to be repeated a few times until the soldier standing behind him was satisfied and told him to proceed to the next name in a harshly modified voice through the helmet's speakers.

At the end of the list, the man was told to look into the camera and speak his own name. As the last syllable left his mouth, a quiet shot was fired and he crumpled to the ground.

Watching the video had been a grueling experience for everyone, but no one would allow themselves to look away. Every person in the rec room stood at rigid attention as the list was read, and they all saluted the last colonist as he was gunned down. Natalia felt a hardened resolve sweeping the ship at this proof of how far the Syndicate was willing to go. Where there had been large numbers of people calling for caution and diplomacy, there was now almost universal support for taking the fight to the Syndicate with the same zeal.

A week after the Mars takeover and two days after the colonist executions, she was watching a live feed of the Coalition Parliament as all three houses met in the same large chamber to vote on a bill. It denounced the Syndicate actions and approved offensive and defensive maneuvers by the Fleet Admiral and Marine Commandant. The vote had been going on for hours, with seemingly every one of the five thousand members of the combined houses wanting to stand and give a speech trumpeting their support for the bill. A few tried to call for a diplomatic resolution to the conflict, but howls and catcalls silenced them quickly.

"It's finally going to happen," Janet said, sitting on the floor at her feet. "We're going to fight back at last."

"About time, too!" someone called from nearby. "You can't let someone keep punching you and hope they'll just get tired of it. You have to punch back."

Nat listened as others chimed in to support the opinion. She felt the same desire to make a move against their opponent, to stop sitting around as if hoping the danger would pass without intervention, but she also felt fear and nervousness. Her sister was on Luna, still refusing to leave Aldrin dome to return to their home on Earth. To compound that, all passenger shuttles were being suspended between the home world and her moon, stranding anyone still on Luna.

The fleet of freighters waited in orbit around the moon, and she knew the Transport Guild would work tirelessly to evacuate as many people as they could. But she also knew that most of them were tied up getting railguns mounted to assist the Coalition frigates in the fight when the Syndicate ships approached Earth. Many of the people there had been born and grown up in Aldrin, and they refused to leave their home for fear of being lost on a planet that was often no more than a blue and green disk in the sky above.

Her reverie was broken as a young ensign rushed into the room. "Attention! Attention! Ship-wide announcement will begin in twenty-three minutes. Please be ready to return to your posts if your commanding officers call you in. Twenty-three minutes!" With those words, the ensign ran out to continue delivering the message. Nat pulled her tablet from where it had slid between the cushion and arm of the chair, and saw a red flash for the urgent message indicator. The same information was displayed there, with a timer counting down. She knew the announcement would be big if they were working so hard to make sure everyone was aware of it.

"Let's get back," she said, nudging Janet with a slippered foot. The two of them rose and said goodbyes to the people around them, walking somberly through the corridors to their cabin. Once inside, both women automatically started pulling off their comfortably loose shirts and pants to get dressed in their jumpsuit and uniform respectively. They went through the motions in total silence, as if afraid to speak and bring bad thoughts to life.

At the very moment the counter on Nat's tablet hit zero, the ship comm trilled loudly. "*Waterloo*, this is Fleet Admiral Holgerson. I am sure many of you have heard the news, but the houses of Parliament voted almost unanimously today to allow action against the Syndicate in retaliation for their heinous attacks against Coalition citizens off world. To that end, at the conclusion of this announcement every frigate in the Navy will be activated. All hands will report to their divisions immediately and prepare for action."

The comms trilled again, and Nat and Janet were left looking at each other in bewilderment. "Are we really doing this?" Janet asked.

"Looks like it, but what exactly are we doing?"

They were interrupted by another ship-wide announcement, the captain ordering everyone to their stations. Outside of the cabin, they headed in opposite directions down the packed corridor. Nat ran as quickly as she could, darting around other people in the crowded passages as everyone tried to make their way to different parts of the frigate. She made it to her Engineering department in twice the amount of time it took walking there at the start of a normal shift. The room was packed with people milling around, a dozen conversations filling the air at once.

Several minutes later, Lieutenant Richtaus appeared above them as she stood on a bench and called out for quiet. The call was repeated around the room a few times until the talking and murmuring died away.

"I know you have a lot of questions," Mags called out loudly so everyone could hear. "I don't have many answers for you. All I can tell you at this moment is that the high and mighty at the top of the ranks are finally getting off their asses and doing something about these Syndicate bastards." A cheer broke out at the words, and the room was filled with loud support for half a minute.

"The captain has ordered everyone to remain at their stations until the all clear sounds or you're sent elsewhere by your commanding officers. Try to stay out of each other's way, and do what you can to get some work done while you're here. If I have more news, I'll share it."

Nat watched the lieutenant disappear into the crowd again, and looked around. No one was doing any work, just chatting with the people around them as they all tried to get another nugget of information that they didn't already know. Suddenly, she felt the deck begin to vibrate beneath her feet, and felt the center of gravity shift a few inches as the frigate increased the power to her engines and changed course.

"Can you believe this?" a voice asked at her elbow, and she turned to see Mags standing beside her. "There was no reason to call everyone out to their stations, just to have them stand around talking."

"It must be important," Nat replied. "Maybe we're finally going to try and head off the Syndicate fleet."

The lieutenant was shaking her head before the words were out. "If that's the case, they would have sent off-duty personnel to their cabins to get into gel beds for a hard burn. This extra bit of thrust is just enough to send us around the planet faster."

The words clicked together in her head, and Nat grunted. "Huh, maybe that's exactly what we're doing. There are two Syndicate frigates still hovering over their capital."

"Ah," Mags said, a smile blossoming. "Yes, that would explain it. I hope that's where we're going, to get some revenge for the people they've killed." The lieutenant was in a bubbly mood as she pushed through the crowd, heading for the grouping of officers deeper in Engineering.

A man who was in her shift appeared. "Do you really think that's what we're doing?" he asked quietly. The prospect didn't seem to give him any joy at all.

Nat shrugged, thinking of her parents and glad they were living in a place far from any important government centers. "Where else would we be going right after Parliament approved an aggressive move forward?"

"Then… that means the ship is about to go into battle. Doesn't that worry you?"

"I spent over a month hooking up thousands of new systems for the *Waterloo.* They just upgraded all our railguns and torpedo launchers, even added on a few more railguns for good measure. I'd say we're more than an even match for any Syndicate frigate." She could see that his expression hadn't lost any of the worry. "Don't forget that we have eight frigates in orbit to their two."

"Ground-based attack," was his simple reply, as he turned to walk away with slumped shoulders. She'd forgotten about the danger of weapons fired from the planet below, but that was mostly because they were highly ineffective against ships in orbit. The technology had been developed thirty years before, at the start of hostilities between the two superpowers, and when it quickly became a cold war with each side maintaining the status quo to prevent one from growing more powerful than the other, those old technologies weren't updated as much as they should have been. As a result, a single frigate could operate with near autonomy in orbit unless an enemy frigate was in the area.

Missiles fired from the surface were a greater threat than ground-to-air railguns, and even then the distances involved provided more than enough warning for the frigates to shoot down or confuse the missiles before they got close to the ship. Small computer-controlled machine guns were mounted in dozens of places across the hull, capable of firing thousands of rounds each minute to guard against attacks from the ground as well as torpedo strikes from another ship or the rare fighter attacks.

Lieutenant Richtaus appeared beside her again, a gleeful grin on the older woman's face. "You were right. We're targeting the Syndicate frigates." Even as she spoke, they felt the deck throb beneath their feet as railguns began to fire. "The admiral wants them both disabled or destroyed, while the other half of the fleet is carrying Marines to Luna to storm Armstrong and take over both domes."

Nat knew she should share the woman's joy at the news, but she still felt the same listless numbness that had been her only emotion since hearing of the deaths of the Deimos colonists. There was a faint concern for her sister, a moment where she hoped that the violence in the lunar domes would not get out of hand.

When the ship was hit by a railgun round several decks above, she and a dozen others were thrown to the ground from the jerking suddenness of halted momentum. Nat scrambled to her feet, and grabbed up a diagnostic and tool kit. She raced away to help repair the damage, patching the smashed hull and bulkheads hit by the round. The sound of railguns and torpedo tubes spitting out their lethal discharges became a constant noise around her as she worked throughout the battle.

Eighteen

Cupping her soft cheek in his hand, Erik leaned down to kiss Dex. Her lips were soft against his, their bodies pressing together as she wrapped both arms around his neck and pulled him close. The kiss went on for what felt like hours, and he wished he could have days or weeks more.

"Get a room, lovebirds," Mira called teasingly as she pushed past to enter the docking tube that led to the *Vagabond.* After three days spent on Luna, the repairs and upgrades were complete and the freighter was ready to clear the pad for another ship to descend from orbit. There were five other ships already on docking platforms in varying stages of shipyard work, all the workers and resources having been pulled away to complete his ship faster than anyone would ever have thought possible.

Three days on Luna, busy days filled with meetings in the Guildhall and working alongside his crew and the shipyard technicians to ensure that work done on the *Vagabond* was completed to Fynn's satisfaction. Nights filled with laughter and nervous joy, as he met with Dex as much as possible outside of their busy work schedules, sharing meals and drinks and kisses.

The night before, his last on Luna until after the coming battle with the Syndicate fleet, she had led him onto a rooftop garden. Hydroponic pillars created columns of greenery around them, as they spread out a blanket and lay looking up at Earth rotating above them. They made love beneath the spinning planet, sharing all of themselves. It was a memory he would hold forever.

“You need to go,” Dex said through a smile as they broke apart.

“They could manage without me,” Erik joked, leaning in to kiss her again.

Laughing, Dex put a hand on his chest and pushed him away. “I’m sure they could, but you’d miss your ship more than you’ll miss me.” She gave him a quick peck on the cheek and then stepped back. “Fly well, Erik, and come back to me when it’s over.”

He stroked a hand along her cheek one more time, drinking in the sight and feel of her while he could. “I’ll see you soon, Dex. I promise you that.” Forcing himself to turn away, he stepped through the hatch into the tube and walked quickly through it to enter the freighter’s airlock. He turned back to wave one last time as the airlock doors irised closed and the docking tube disconnected with a puff of air.

Turning reluctantly after he watched Dex walk away, Erik made his way through the corridors of the ship. The work on the hull was virtually undetectable from inside the ship, aside from a smell of ozone left behind from all the welding of new hull plating. Isaac had spent the last two days on the ship, running wiring and coding programs to control the new railgun on the belly of the ship. Jen had found excuses to be aboard at the same time, to the amusement of the others. They’d lost a bit of space in the cargo bay to make room for the gun mounts, but the

Vagabond was now ready to rain depleted uranium on the Syndicate cruiser.

President Meyers had even managed to get them a crate with several dozen additional rounds for the guns, though he had been tight lipped about where or how he got them. The news from Mars had put a damper on the growing enthusiasm, but it also steeled the resolve of everyone involved to get the freighters armed and ready for the conflict to come.

Entering the control room, he found Mira at the pilot station communicating with Luna's AI to get authorization to depart. He strapped into his command chair, closing his eyes to take a few moments to relive his nights with Dex. A smile spread across his lips, and he could almost smell her scent on the air and feel her fingers on his skin.

"Ready to go, cap." Mira was turned around and staring at him with a wide grin. He had a feeling she'd been talking to him for a few minutes.

"Take us up," he said, feeling his face turn red. He flicked the switch for the ship's comms. "Thirty seconds to departure."

Mira was chuckling at her station as her fingers flew across the screens in front of her. The engines flared to life, and the ship started a subtle vibration that no one aboard registered after so many years of living on ships in flight. "Did you hear about the Parliament vote today?" she asked.

Erik pulled up a news scroll on his display, and saw a line about the vote to approve aggressive action against the Syndicate forces. The votes were being taken and the scroll was updating the results as they came in. "Looks like they're finally going to do something besides huddle around Earth."

"Let's hope we get in on some of that action," the pilot said wolfishly. "I want to deal some payback for the friends I've lost to those evil bastards."

"I have no doubts they'll use us, especially now that the freighters are being armed." Erik pulled up the stats on the retrofits he had received from the Guild. "We're the seventh to be completed and armed, and by the end of the week there should be four more. Enough of us to more than hold our own against a frigate."

The *Vagabond* rose above the two domes, and Erik watched the view from the ventral cameras as the light from the sun reflected off the silvery glass on the top of Aldrin and Armstrong. It was a majestic sight. He couldn't help but wonder how the people who had managed to build such magnificent structures, capable of holding back the dangers of the vacuum, couldn't manage to keep from trying to assert dominance over each other.

They were halfway to orbit when there was a bright flash from the camera. The light was intense enough that the view went black for several seconds before coming back up. The docking platforms below were a tangled mess of steel and plastic. A small crater had appeared where the six platforms had been a minute before. The *Vagabond* shuddered as the shockwave from the blasts passed through the ship, and red warning lights began to flash across the displays as warning tones started to sound insistently.

"What the hell just happened?" Mira yelled.

"I think someone just blew up the docks," Erik said in stunned disbelief. There was no sign of the dozens of workers who had been swarming over the ships, and he knew that there would have been crew members aboard each freighter helping with the retrofitting work. "Did we take any damage?"

"Only minor impacts to the hull," she told him, fingers flying across the screens faster than he could track. "If we'd left only a few seconds later, though…."

"Yeah, then we'd have been in real trouble." The thin atmosphere of the moon had saved them, with the explosion below throwing debris in all directions instead of containing the blast in a solely upward cone. Erik cycled through several alert screens, dismissing them as he resolved any issues or found them to be informational only. By the time the control room was silent again with the last of the alarms being dealt with, the *Vagabond* was ready to enter orbit around Luna.

A connection request had been flashing on the screen for most of a minute, and he finally had a chance to tap the button to accept the call. Dex appeared, the view around her jerking around as she ran through the streets. "Erik, thank God. Are you okay?"

"We're fine, just minor damage from debris hitting us from below. What happened?"

"It looks like it could be the same bomber who hit Earth last month. President Meyers got a message only seconds before the bombs went off, some kind of rambling anti-off-world manifesto. I have to go, I'm almost at the Guildhall and we have a lot to deal with. I just wanted to know you were safe."

He smiled faintly at her, and touched the screen in front of him. "I'm fine, Dex. You stay safe down there. If the bomber hit the docks then it means they're on Luna."

"I know," she said grimly, her jaw clenching. "I'll contact you when I can."

The connection closed and the screen returned to a row of status reports. Erik tied into the channel shared between the orbiting freighters, to hear a cacophony of voices as the other eleven ships were all talking at once. He tried to make out the separate conversational threads, but gave up after a few seconds. He knew that one of the ships had been starting a descent to land on the pad that his ship had just vacated, and the rest of the ships seemed to be asking for news or offering wild theories about the explosions.

"Mira, any chance the Coalition is sending out any information or updates? Those were their docks that just got bombed, after all."

"Nothing on that yet, cap." Her voice was hesitant, and she paused before throwing up an image on the main holo display at the front of the room. He could see the gentle curve of Earth set against the blackness of space, and several ships with flaring engines making their way around the planet. "Four of the Coalition frigates changed course just a few minutes ago and it looks like they're on an intercept course with the Syndicate frigates. The remainder of the fleet is burning for Luna, but they started before the explosion so I don't know what their purpose is."

"It appears the action is definitely about to start. Coordinate with the Guild to find out what's going on below, and have the computer sift through news reports." With the freighter in a stable orbit, Erik unstrapped and left the control room to hurry through the corridors. He poked his head in the medical bay and found Jen and Isaac going through all the new supplies that had been loaded onto the ship during the hull refit. "Everything okay, doc? No injuries?"

"Not so much as a scratch reported," she said. "Do you think it's the Earth bomber?"

News had traveled fast, and he had no doubt that the crew had been tapping into the news reports even while he was working to clear warning messages and talking with Dex. "I would say that's the safe assumption at the moment. It'll probably be a few days before we find out anything concrete."

The technician turned with a fearful expression. "What about the other ships that were docked? Did anyone survive?"

"It didn't look good, Isaac." Erik sighed. "I don't think anyone would survive the mess I saw after the explosion. If they did, the Guild will work to get them into the dome and patched up."

Continuing along the corridor, he passed through the reactor room and entered the engine room. Fynn was cursing softly at the screen in front of him, flipping back and forth between two different reports.

"Any systems get screwed up from the blast debris?"

"No, thankfully." The engineer shook his head in disgust. "We have a lot of dents in our shiny new hull plates, though. It looks like there are a few micro fractures that I'm going to have to go out and repair. Nothing that's going to cause issues, but if we get into a situation that requires a heavy burn or an excessive amount of evasive maneuvers then I don't want some weak spots turning into problems at the worst moment."

"He means *I'll* have to go out and make the repairs," Tom said, poking his head up from behind the central console where he had been doing some maintenance. "I'll need a couple of hours for it."

Erik nodded, typing in a short reminder on his tablet. "I'll let you guys know as soon as that can be done. I'd like to find out what exactly happened first, and see what's going on with the Coalition frigates." He explained about the fleet of frigates splitting up, with half of them burning hard for Luna. "Should be here in a little over an hour at the rate they're moving."

Returning to the control room after checking in on Isaac, he heard Mira talking quietly and then falling silent as she listened to someone in her earpiece. Erik strapped back into his command chair and started checking the systems for updated status reports and any new information.

"Thanks for the news, Ben. Yeah, it's good to be back." Mira pressed a button to end her communication, and flipped her chair around to face him. “That was an old friend who’s on the frigate *Waterloo*. One of the guys who showed me the ropes when I first decided to be a pilot. He said he couldn’t share much with me, but the Fleet Admiral is taking the new resolution from Parliament to heart. Without confirming it, he let me know that they’re about to engage the two Syndicate frigates that are orbiting over Hong Kong.”

Erik pumped a fist in the air. “It’s about time! What about the ships headed this way?”

She shook her head and shrugged. “He wasn’t sure what they might be doing. Sounds like the command staff over there is being pretty tight lipped about their plans. Ben said they didn’t even know about the explosions on the Aldrin docking pads until I told him.”

Looking at the display that still showed four frigates moving around Earth, he tapped his fingers as he considered their options. “Put in a request to the Guildhall. I want to break from orbit and see if we can join those ships. There’s no chance to get there before they engage the Syndicate ships, but even watching the action will help us know their tactics in the future.”

“Will do, cap.” Mira turned and started placing calls, working through several layers of bureaucracy. Ten minutes later, they had the permissions they needed and Erik gave the command to burn for Earth. He was surprised when four other freighters followed, their captains sending messages that they were ordered to follow in case of any trouble. He felt a bit of pride at the feeling that the Transport Guild had just unofficially created their first defensive fleet.

It took them an hour and a half to reach Earth, the rotation of the planet bringing the Syndicate ships closer as they approached. Twenty minutes out, he and Mira watched on the screen as the four Coalition frigates approached the two Syndicate frigates. It almost seemed as if both sides started to fire at the same moment, railgun rounds flashing out with torpedoes flaring toward their targets. It was an awe-inspiring display of firepower, and the *Vagabond* crew could only watch as the freighter slowed to maintain a safe distance.

The Coalition group was led by a ship with a transponder signal of *Waterloo*. Erik could see the shiny seams around weapon emplacements that told him this ship had gone through its own round of upgrades recently. The forward railguns spat out rounds toward the enemy ships, brief flashes as they exited the guns. Mira at first had the ship's computer track and highlight each round, but as the other ships joined in the screen was filled with too much color, obscuring everything else. She canceled the program and they watched for the telltale flashes of the railguns firing.

Within seconds, the rounds were tearing into the Syndicate frigates even as rounds fired from those ships were tearing into the Coalition frigates. Debris from the ships was ejecting into space, some falling through the planet's atmosphere and creating fiery flashes. The spread of torpedoes between the two groups were taken out by railgun rounds or smaller weaponry made for the purpose, the warheads flashing as they exploded and adding to the chaotic action on the screen. The Coalition frigates continued to advance, closing the distance until the lead vessel passed between the enemy ships.

Erik watched in awe as both Syndicate frigates focused their fire on the *Waterloo*, the distance between the ships small enough for almost instantaneous impact as the guns fired. Round after round impacted the hull and threw out debris and atmosphere, and he began to wonder if the ship's captain had made a fatal error. The *Waterloo* returned fire, the heavy barrage bursting through the Syndicate ships and sending several rounds through the other side of the vessels. Seconds later, rounds impacted the bow of the Syndicate frigates as the other Coalition ships had taken the opportunity to focus their fire unopposed.

Mira gasped as the first Syndicate frigate exploded, a quick flash of light followed by the vessel being torn into four different sections. The *Waterloo* continued to pour furious fire into the remaining enemy ship, her engines flaring as the ship was pushed forward and away from the planet below to get out of the path of the growing debris field. The frigate was opening a gap as the second Syndicate ship took multiple rounds to her engines.

Light faded as the engines died.

The Syndicate frigate seemed to groan with despair as her bow dipped from the rounds that continued to hammer into her from the other Coalition ships.

Erik and Mira watched in complete silence as the ship succumbed to gravity, flames engulfing the bow of the ship as it passed into Earth's atmosphere. The hull had been so weakened from the rounds that hammered it, the ship broke apart under the stress of re-entry. A dozen chunks of the vessel fell through the sky until they crashed into the planet below in fiery explosions.

The *Waterloo* was wounded after the battle, penetrated by dozens of rounds during its brave assault on the enemy ships. The three other frigates surrounded her as they all burned to return to orbit over Coalition territory. Having seen battle for the first time outside of simulations, Erik was speechless with the ferocity of the display. It had been barely half an hour from the first shots to the total destruction of the Syndicate frigates, an unexpected show of overwhelming force.

NINETEEN

During the short battle, Nat remained in her Engineering section surrounded by work crews from the three shifts all clustered together. Now and then, news would trickle in and be shouted around to update everyone as they felt the ship shudder with each round fired by a railgun. The firing had been so fast and furious that she had felt as if the ship were trying to vibrate her skin from her bones, teeth rattling together until she clenched her jaw so hard that the muscles still hurt days later.

When the *Waterloo* began her daring run between the enemy ships, the group huddled around her had been unaware of it until depleted uranium rounds began to fire through their section of the ship. Nat watched as two people only steps away from her became a mist of blood and flesh when a round passed through the bulkhead and continued farther into the ship.

Screaming and terror erupted, everyone pushing to try and get out of the area as those spattered by the gore were yelling in shock and disgust. It was the impetus she needed, breaking her from stunned numbness. Events snapped into sharp focus as the reality of the situation crashed upon her.

She rushed forward against the flow of people running away, kneeling at the side of a woman who had fallen in the crush and been stepped on by panicked crew members. Nat checked the blood on the woman's face, finding a cut on her scalp that was bleeding profusely but wasn't serious. She helped the woman to her feet, yelled at her to get to medical, and then pushed against the flow again.

The next person she found was her lieutenant, leaning against a bulkhead with a white face as she clutched at a shoulder where her arm ended in ragged strips of flesh and muscle.

"Mags," she shouted over the sounds of hysteria around them. "We need to get you to a doctor." Nat looked around and stepped over to pull a first aid kit from the wall. Opening it, she found a plastic tourniquet and tied it around the officer's shoulder to staunch the blood flowing freely from the wound. Once that was done, she injected an ampoule of morphine to dull the pain Mags had to be feeling even though she'd made no sound and continued staring into space.

"We need to move, Mags. Let's get you up." Nat wrapped the woman's good arm over her shoulder and placed her own arm around the woman's back, pulling her up to a standing position. The room had cleared of the panicked people, and she managed to get the lieutenant to take a few halting steps. She was supporting most of Mags' weight as they walked, and it was a relief to see two of the medical crew rush into the Engineering section.

The men stopped to stare in stunned disbelief at the spray of blood and flesh on the floor and walls, but snapped their attention to the struggling Nat quickly. They helped her get Mags onto a floating stretcher, and one of the nurses started to work on the wound as the other pushed the stretcher out of the room toward the nearest medical bay.

Nat started to follow behind, but then looked around the empty room and realized that there was work to be done and she had to take the initiative. She rushed over to check the hole in the bulkhead where the railgun round had passed through. Shocked, she realized she could still hear the rounds passing through the ship in other sections nearby, the battle raging around them. The hull would have sealed itself as the round passed through, designed for battle situations such as this.

A console nearby was flashing with alert messages, automated damage reports as well as those being sent in from other departments across the frigate. Nat pulled up the reports and saw a request from the bridge taking priority over all other work. She grabbed a diagnostic kit and ran through the corridors. The bridge was seven decks above, but she couldn't trust the lifts in the midst of battle and had to climb stairways where she could. Stairwells spread across the ship would traverse three levels at the most, often only two, as a defensive measure to prevent boarders from moving quickly through the ship.

By the time she approached the bridge, she could feel the ship firing rounds at a furious pace and being struck just as often. Twice she passed through sections of the ship as they were hit, and felt the momentary pull of air being sucked into space before the hull sealed itself to maintain pressurization.

She found the multilevel bridge in chaos, crew members at stations calling out reports and updates at a frantic pace as officers rushed around. The captain and admiral were standing with calm poses on the command deck above, their eyes moving from station to station as they caught bits of reports and received updates from officers who approached.

“You from Engineering?” a man nearby asked her, and she nodded. “Thank God someone made it up here. I’ve been asking for assistance for a long time! Several of our most critical stations were damaged in the first rounds from the Syndicate frigates.” He ushered her to a large console with a dozen screens arrayed for three people to monitor, all of them black as the console was left without power. “This is the sensor station. We have people down in the technical department having to manually relay information up to us, so do what you can to get this station working.”

The man hurried away, leaving Nat to stare around at the frantic activity on the bridge. Steadying herself with a deep breath, she opened the kit and pulled out a tool to open the panels at the base of the console so she could access the wiring and diagnostic relays within. As she worked, she kept her ears attuned to the noise around her. She was able to pick out individual voices now and then, hearing snippets of reports about areas of the ship damaged in the return fire from the Syndicate vessels. She learned of their position between the two as she listened, almost slamming her head against the metal above her as she jerked in shock.

Another voice nearby shouted out in alarm, and she felt the ship jerk around her as if a giant had grabbed hold and given it a vigorous shake. The diagnostic tool she’d been holding was thrown out of the small space and her head cracked against the wall as her arms got tangled in the wiring.

“Get us out of the debris field!” she heard someone call out, unsure if it was the captain, admiral, or perhaps some other officer unafraid to give the order. The ship began to thrum as the engines flared and she felt an increase of gravity as the *Waterloo* surged forward and up. Pulling herself out of the space under the sensor station console, she could see the shattered remnants of one of the Syndicate frigates displayed on a screen nearby. Another showed the second enemy ship, railguns pouring rounds into it as the *Waterloo* moved away.

The admiral was leaning on a rail above, blood streaming down his face from a wound he must have sustained in the shockwave from the destroyed ship. “Focus fire on the remaining frigate,” he yelled needlessly.

Nat could feel her heart beating fast in her chest, adrenaline pulsing through her veins. She turned back to the console she was supposed to be working on, looking around to find the diagnostic tool and grab it from the deck several feet away. Crawling back into the tangle of wires, she connected the tool to the diagnostic relay and waited a few seconds for the display to show the possible location of the issue. A string of numbers and letters appeared on the screen, locations of half a dozen wires and connections that were reporting errors or no connection at all.

She had repaired a couple of the issues and was working on the third when the deck shuddered again and several people cried out on the bridge. Pulling her head out from under the console once again, she watched in open-mouthed awe as the second Syndicate ship broke apart and dropped through the planet’s atmosphere in flaming chunks.

The bridge crew broke out in a cheer as they watched the display. Nat cheered along with them, feeling joy at the thought that she'd been a part of the attack that was finally taking revenge for the losses they'd all suffered over the previous few months. They were fighting back against the threat that had been looming since the revelation of the Syndicate cruiser.

In the days after the battle, the *Waterloo* had limped away to safety from the missiles and railgun rounds being fired from the surface of the planet. The crew set about the arduous task of making repairs. Thirty-four crew members had lost their lives in the fight, an astonishingly low number considering the number of rounds that had passed into and through the frigate. Another eighty-three were injured, with a dozen critical enough to go either way.

Lieutenant Richtaus was still in the medical bay, her arm removed at the shoulder so that a bio-plastic replacement could be fitted. She would be kept from duty for several weeks as she went through nerve regeneration and physical therapy to learn to use the new appendage, and the Chief Engineer had decided to give Nat the temporary job of filling in for the officer.

Being in charge of a team that consisted of seven other engineering crew proved to be the balm she needed. Doing her own work while also keeping track of the others, swinging by to check in on their jobs and offering advice where needed, kept her mind busy so that she didn't think about the battle or her sister still being on Luna where the bomber had struck. Finding out about those explosions and the lost freighters and shipyard workers had killed any joy from destroying the Syndicate frigates. It was proof that no matter what small victories they achieved, this wouldn't be over until one side or the other was completely knocked out.

"Boss," a voice said in her ear. She wore the comm piece at all times when she was on duty now, open to the channel shared between her team.

"I'm here, Rafferty. What's up?"

"Um, the captain is down here in Engineering, asking for you. Chief's talking with him now, but you might want to start heading this way."

Sighing loudly, she stopped her forward progress and turned to backtrack the course she'd been following for the last five minutes. "Be there in ten." Nat wondered what the captain could possibly want with her. She had stayed on the bridge right after the battle to complete repairs on the sensor station, bringing it up to full functionality before she was satisfied and would leave it to move to the next urgent repair that was waiting. Hopefully some wire hadn't come loose in the tangle and she wasn't on her way for a dressing down about a problem that she didn't cause.

The Chief Engineer broke into her group's channel to ask her to return a few minutes later, and she jogged where possible to move quicker. There had been a breathless quality in the chief's voice that she'd never heard before.

Rushing into the Engineering substation she was based in, she found the Chief Engineer and the *Waterloo's* captain talking while half a dozen of her coworkers loitered around them trying not to be obvious in their eavesdropping.

Rafferty, the crewman who had first warned her, was standing by an open locker and tossed her a thumbs up as she entered.

Brow furrowed, she came to a stop in front of the captain and came as close as she ever could to a sharp salute. Shows of that nature were more for the command staff and officer corps, while the average member of the crew found it demeaning to always have to give a salute when called before an officer.

"This is Natalia Avila, sir," the chief said, patting her on the shoulder with a heavy hand. "One of our best down here in Engineering."

The captain nodded and stood erect with his hands in the small of his back. "Miss Avila, I have been hearing your name quite often the last several weeks, so I thought it was about time I met you in person."

"Sir?" she asked in surprise, trying to figure out why her name would be anywhere near the captain of the ship.

Captain Andrews smiled, setting her at ease slightly. "Lieutenant Richtaus has been with me on every boat for the last ten years, so she and I have become friendly and often share a drink in the lounge. She's spoken highly of you, says that you're one of the few that she can always count on to get the work done right and on time."

A shadow crossed his face. "It was a shock to hear that she was hit by one of the railgun rounds, but had it not been for your quick thinking with a tourniquet I'm told she would likely have lost too much blood and could have died.

"On top of that, you were the one to keep a cool head and answer the call on the bridge for urgent repairs. The fact that you made your way through the ship in the middle of a battle speaks volumes about your courage, Miss Avila. I would be proud to serve with you at any time." His hands appeared from behind his back, holding a small box. The captain held it forward, opening the lid to reveal a small round white pip that looked much like one of the four on the captain's chest that denoted his rank.

"As part of the war powers act, a ship's commanding officer is allowed to make battlefield promotions to reward extraordinary service. I can think of few who would deserve it as much as you do, *Ensign* Avila, and the admiral is in full agreement."

Nat's eyes had grown larger with every word, and she could only stare down at the pip she'd never thought it would be possible to wear. Non-commissioned officer ranks had been the extent of her dreams, the square rank badges that set them apart from the officer corps. She tried to swallow, but her mouth felt as dry as a desert as she raised her eyes to meet the captain's. "Thank you, sir," she croaked.

Captain Andrews chuckled softly, pulling out the white circle and clipping it to her uniform as the rest of the room broke out in applause and whistles. With shaking fingers, she reached up to rub at the smooth enameled surface of the rank pip. She felt a beaming smile spread across her face as she shook hands with the captain.

TWENTY

Anders entered the briefing room, and threw a fist against the wall. Davis looked up, one brow raised inquiringly. "What is it, sergeant?"

"The bastards destroyed our frigates, sir. Both of them completely smashed, everyone aboard killed. More than fourteen thousand dead from the impacts when the second ship fell from orbit."

Davis took a deep breath, leaning back in the chair and steadying himself. He had expected retaliation for the attack on Mars, but not something this big. "How many ships did the Coalition lose?"

"None," Anders spat. "Observers say that one of the frigates took heavy damage, but the others were barely scratched."

"Well, I should say I'm surprised even one of their ships was damaged. Eight against two are not good odds."

"Four against two. The other frigates were seen heading to Luna." Anders sat in one of the chairs that the assault soldiers filled during briefings, a grim smile spreading across his face. "Looks like the bomber is back, and he destroyed the docking complex at Aldrin. The reports I've seen are a bit slim on actual information, but we know there were explosions there."

Davis was even more surprised at this news. When the first bomb went off in New York, he had shared the conviction of many on the *Indomitable* that the Syndicate had been funding the attacks. With the Coalition being targeted with each blast, he had been more positive. However, when the bombings stopped and the Syndicate committees still didn't take credit or even let it be known amongst their own senior officers, he had begun to question his conviction. Undoubtedly, there had to be many groups on Earth that would be more than willing to take advantage of the chaos of the situation to try and force their own agenda. It was even possible that each attack could be the work of a different person or group.

Turning to the terminal on his desk, he pulled up the latest reports trickling down from the cruiser's command staff. He saw a mention of Coalition ships approaching their frigates over Hong Kong, but nothing about an attack on Luna. The latest report was more than half an hour old, even after he put in a refresh request with the ship's servers.

He was closing out of the terminal when a message with the highest urgency level appeared on the screen. "I've been summoned to the admiral," he told his sergeant, rising to pull his tunic and remove any wrinkles from long hours of sitting at the desk. "I don't know how long I'll be, so run the team through more ship boarding sessions. I feel certain that will be our next mission now that the Coalition seems to have found some spine."

The assault team's quarters and training area were far from the bridge and the admiral's office, so it took half an hour to traverse the cruiser and arrive outside the door. Two Marines stood beside it on sentry duty, each carrying a lethal flechette rifle at attention across their chest. It was an action that signified the ship was at war, the Marines given permission to fire as necessary if someone tried to forcefully enter the admiral's office or bridge. One of the men saluted, and Davis snapped his hand to his temple in reply.

"The admiral is expecting you, sir."

"Thank you, Marine." Davis waved his hand over the sensor and waited a few seconds as authorization was granted from within and the door hissed open. Once inside the large room, more spacious than the cabins that two to four crew members shared throughout the cruiser, he found the admiral sitting at a large desk reading reports on a curving holo display. Davis snapped to attention, presenting a sharp salute. "Reporting as ordered, admiral."

"Lieutenant, please sit." Admiral Yumata pressed a button to turn off the displays, and swiveled to face Davis. "Excellent work on Deimos, by the way. Your team performed admirably, and I have noted in my reports to the Military Committee that you should all be commended. Not one Syndicate citizen harmed, and only minor damage to the airlock and warehouse facility. A much better result than the original plan, though we did still confiscate almost all hydroponics equipment. The colonies must be dependent upon Earth again, to maintain our control over them."

"Thank you, sir. My team followed through on the plan exactly as we rehearsed."

Clasping his hands together on the desk, Yumata leaned forward. "Have you heard about the attack on our frigates in Earth orbit?"

“Sergeant Anders told me about it just before I received your summons, sir. Such a move had to be expected after our actions on Mars.”

“Yes, it should have been,” the admiral sniffed. “Such a possibility was in the brief I sent to the Military Committee, but they choose to believe the Coalition would continue holding firm in a defensive posture. Now they’re also making moves to secure Luna.”

Davis stiffened. “How so, sir?”

“Four of their frigates have entered orbit around the moon, with the freighter trash they are desperately arming. Our sources tell us that Marines will be landed as soon as the docking facilities can be repaired.” Yumata smiled with satisfaction. “Whoever bombed them not only destroyed the landing pads and docking facility, but they also obliterated five of the freighters that were having railguns mounted. If we ever find out who’s doing that, we should give them a commission to serve the Syndicate.”

Davis considered the information. “They should be able to jury rig something within a few days, sir, and begin dropping their Marines. Will the Military Committee send more Marines to Armstrong to help defend against the incursion?”

“No, the frigates have arranged themselves to cover any approach. Our troop transports have light weapons for ground assaults, not ship-to-ship battles. It would be a slaughter.”

“How many are in the garrison of Armstrong dome, sir? It can’t be more than a handful of squads.”

"I believe there are six, with two majors in charge of the operations."

"Fifty Marines," Davis mused. "The Coalition will send in several hundred, perhaps a thousand, to sweep away any resistance."

A challenging light appeared in the admiral's eyes, and he smiled. "How would you handle the defense, lieutenant?"

"I've only been on Luna a few times, no more than a couple of days each time as I changed ships for new assignments." Lips pursed, Davis paused to picture the layout of the two domes in his head. Surprisingly, he knew more of Aldrin than Armstrong since he'd spent most of his time in the Coalition dome sampling the entertainment options there. He narrowed his focus to the long underground tunnel that connected the domes. "I would hope that the checkpoint at the dome entry has a stun field. Two, if I had set it up, one in front of the guard post and one behind. That would be the first line of defense, with Marines firing from behind cover as the Coalition troops approach. With proper leadership and a bit of luck, our troops could inflict several dozen casualties on the enemy before they are overrun, and the stun fields would slow the advance.

"My memory is of a tight street at the entry point to the dome from the tunnel, a perfect place to create fallback positions and keep up a steady fire on the Coalition soldiers. The rooftops would provide vantage points that could give devastating effect if used properly." Davis grimaced as the battle played out in his head. "Armstrong administration would try to prevent it, but I would bring down buildings at side streets to extend the single approach for as long as possible. The rubble would also give opportunity to place mines and focused claymores that could be activated by motion or remote detonation. Done properly, the enemy will have lost a couple of hundred soldiers at this point, though I would fully expect to lose half of our own. Such ferocity in defense would also slow their advance."

"Excellent tactics so far," the admiral said quietly. "What happens when the Coalition troops are out of this funnel of death?"

"At that point, sir, the fight is well and truly lost. I'd advise my Marines to take shelter where they can within the dome, melt into the populace, and look for opportunities to strike from the shadows. Place improvised explosive devices where the enemy tends to cluster, sabotage their equipment if possible, poison their rations. It would be a war of attrition at that point, but each small victory would give heart to the citizens within Armstrong. It would keep them strong in their support of the Syndicate as we work to reclaim our rightful position and eject the Coalition from both domes and the planet below."

Admiral Yumata raised his eyebrows. "This is something I did not expect to hear from you, lieutenant. Are you not the one who always urges caution and acceptance of the enemy's viewpoints?"

"Yes, sir, that has always been my position. Until recently. The Coalition's actions are proving that they have no regard for our people. Attacking our frigates is one thing, but letting the shattered remains fall to the planet and kill countless civilians is too far. Arming freighters is just as bad, a group that is supposed to be neutral in all respects."

"Mmmm.... The Transport Guild will need to go, of course. I have the full backing of the Military Committee on that, and one of our first actions after reclaiming Luna will be to track down and execute any member of that institution. They made the mistake of choosing a side in the war, and then choosing the wrong side."

Davis felt his lips quirk up in a smile as he focused on the admiral's words. "We'll go to Luna, sir?"

"Yes, lieutenant. Our work on Mars is complete. The planet and its moons are fully under Syndicate control. We have made a strong statement that our power cannot be resisted. I will give the order in a few hours to set course for Luna. I fully expect the Coalition frigates will finally advance to meet us as we approach."

"Sir, I'd like to ask permission to use my team to assault an enemy frigate. Ghost Squad is ready to infiltrate and destroy, and I feel confident that we can use our skills and training to strongly hinder their effectiveness at the very least."

"This brings me to the reason for calling you to my office, lieutenant. Our sources in the Coalition government have passed information that their Fleet Admiral has stationed himself on one of their frigates. This gives us a stellar opportunity to cut the head from the snake and stomp the rest as it writhes."

Yumata smiled, relishing the thought. "It will take us nineteen days to reach Earth and Luna, but if the Coalition moves to intercept as I expect, then we should be in battle within two weeks at the most. I plan to launch your team in the insertion pods a day in advance, to give you time to work. I want you to kill their admiral. The captain of the frigate as well, if possible."

Davis stood and snapped a sharp salute. "Admiral, my men will be ready when the time comes. I thank you for your confidence in our abilities. We will do as requested, have no doubts."

"Excellent, lieutenant. Do this job well, and I feel certain I can finally force through a promotion to captain. I'm tired of the Marine command refusing to advance you just because I coerced them to let you work for me."

"It is an honor to work with you, sir, whatever rank I have."

"We will do great things together, lieutenant. Great things." The admiral nodded in satisfaction, and then waved a hand. "Dismissed. Get your team prepped for their mission."

Davis saluted again, and then turned and strode from the room. As he walked through the corridors to return to his team's section of the ship, he felt joy at the prospect of the mission ahead. He would still have to decide which of the team would remain behind since they were one pod short, but felt confident that nine members of the team would be more than enough to infiltrate the Coalition frigate and eliminate their admiral. With a bit of luck, they could cause a great deal of chaos in the enemy fleet and disrupt them enough to allow the *Indomitable* to easily wipe the last resistance away.

TWENTY ONE

The *Vagabond* had spent a week in orbit around Luna, the freighters clustering around the four Coalition frigates that still watched as repairs were made to the docking facilities for Aldrin. The leader of the work crew on the surface of the moon had assured the captains of the frigates that he could have the docks ready to receive the Marine shuttles within two days, three at the most.

That had been before the constant sabotages that set back the process almost every day and left them no more than halfway to completion so many days later. So far the Marines on the ground had been unable to determine who was working against the process, but felt sure it was a Syndicate spy from Armstrong dome.

Erik was starting to feel impatient with the government establishment, frustrated that the Coalition military chose to see Syndicate spies or saboteurs behind every little malady and issue. He had floated the idea that the Marines could put on pressure suits and then be dropped off by the shuttles on the surface of Luna for a short walk to enter the docking facility that was still exposed to the vacuum of space. But he'd been told to stay out of the discussions. The frigate captains were making it very clear that they felt the freighter crews were untrained hindrances to the war effort, no matter how many railguns they carried.

Unfortunately, that was not as many as they had hoped for. Only eight of the twelve freighters in orbit had been armed, with four awaiting their turn before the shipyards were destroyed. They had enough firepower to be the equivalent to a frigate, however, a powerful addition to the defense of Earth and Luna. That was without including the two other ships that had been given the same heavy railguns as the *Vagabond*, capable of firing a fifty kilo slug at twice the speed of the lighter variety.

His display chimed, alerting him to an incoming message. Erik tapped the screen to open it, smiling when he saw that the message came from Dex. *Erik, Meyers said it's time to put the plan in place. The Syndicate cruiser left Mars three days ago, and the Coalition fleet will be departing within the week to meet them at a safe distance from Earth. Stay safe. I have lots of kisses saved up for when you're back on Luna. By the way, Robert's research was right. The team on Deimos sent a copy of their work before the colony was "sanitized", and the team on Earth was able to combine that with their work to clear the hurdles. They're starting to build a prototype.*

Erik felt elated at the news. As long as the Syndicate cruiser could be stopped, the system would receive a fantastic gift to honor the memory of a man who had worked in anonymous obscurity on an asteroid mining colony most of his life. He would make sure that everyone knew who was responsible for the new technology when it was introduced.

"We just got the thumbs up," he said to Mira.

"Time for a little of the old razzle dazzle?" she asked with a grin.

"I have no idea what that is, so I'm going to say yes and not even ask what you think you just said."

"Aye aye, cap." She punched a few buttons, and the *Vagabond*'s thrusters fired. Slowly, they broke away from the orbiting vessels. Erik passed the word to the rest of the crew, watching on the cameras as everyone strapped in to a crash couch somewhere on the ship. Then he gave Mira the okay.

"Let's see what this old girl can do with her makeover," the pilot said, throwing the engines up to a three G burn within a minute. The rattles and shaking that had been a fact of life aboard the repurposed ship since Erik was eleven years old were no more. The ship accelerated smoothly, with only the faint vibrations he remembered from his years on a Coalition frigate.

"Push her a bit harder," he told Mira through the strain of the pressure pushing him back into the gel of his chair. She whooped and pushed the slider forward half an inch more, and the ship jumped forward to five G's. If not for the increased gravity, Erik would have thought the ship was barely moving at all.

"Looks like that new frame and hull plating was worth the fortune spent getting it all installed so quickly," Mira called out. They watched on the main display as the bow camera showed Earth growing larger and then fading away as they passed above the planet. Their course would take them several million kilometers beyond it, to where two other ships waited in the sensor shadow of the planet. They could remain undetected by the approaching Syndicate fleet.

As they neared the rendezvous point, Mira cut power to the rear thrusters and funneled energy to the braking thrusters that would slow them enough over the next hour to remain in the correct orbit. Erik saw transponder pings come in from the two other freighters, the *Cambier* and the *Montford* waiting for his arrival. He pinged them back quickly, using the accepted signal to let them know that the correct ship approached and that the plan was now in motion.

Dex sent the message off to Erik, already starting to worry about him. The Guildhall was quieter today. Many of the workers who had been spending most of their waking hours there since the news from Interamnia were now too afraid to leave their supposedly safe houses. A wave of growing paranoia had swept Aldrin, with people convinced that the explosion at the docks had not only hindered the Coalition war effort but also trapped the mad bomber inside the dome with them. Those who hadn't left Luna in the early days were often regretting it now that there was no way off the moon.

Dex had tried to reassure several of her friends that the bomber had most likely left Luna before the explosives went off, or had gone to Armstrong dome where he could stay without being accosted, but none of them would believe it.

President Meyers was a few desks away, head leaning on a hand as he tried to convince the Coalition authorities once more to land their Marines on the surface of the planet and walk them through the bombed out area in pressure suits. She had often heard him muttering about the ineptitude of bureaucratic military structures. The major his calls kept being routed to would only repeat the command decision to hold back the troop landings until the Aldrin docking facilities could be repaired to allow for at least one shuttle at a time.

"Okay, but what about landing on the Armstrong pads and storming the docking facility there?" Meyers' tone was resigned as he spoke the words, knowing he'd be told once again that the casualties suffered during the maneuver would be too high.

Dex pulled up the list of communications coming in from the freighters in orbit above, mostly requests for information the Guildhall might have received about the advance of the Syndicate fleet. Some did ask when they would get weapons mounted on their ships, but for the most part those who had been left unarmed by the sabotage seemed relieved that they would have an excuse to duck out of a fight. The short battle between frigates above Earth had been only partially visible from Luna, starting over the horizon from them, but what they had seen was a ferocious assault that had dulled the warmongering fires in many of the freighter captains.

"No, I don't know who keeps sabotaging the work being done on the repairs," Meyers yelled out, the frustration starting to show through. "Maybe if we had some Marines down here to keep an eye on the repairs, then saboteurs couldn't sneak in at night and undo most of the work!"

Fighting laughter, Dex turned away. Meyers had tried to get the Marine guards already in the dome to start watching over the docking facility, but the commander of the three squads said his soldiers were too busy with the guard station in the transfer tunnel. Even one or two Marines a night was apparently out of the question, with the focus being so tight on the Syndicate troops in the other dome to the exclusion of all else.

A long, low rumble shook the Guildhall. Everyone went quiet as they looked around for the source of the disruption. President Meyers looked up from the video call. He stepped quickly to the door of the hall, opening it to look out into the square. In the distance, they could see a gray haze on the air. People nearby were screaming and running in the opposite direction. Meyers grabbed one of them, asking what had happened.

"The tunnel," the terrified woman yelled. "Someone blew up the tunnel!" She tore her sleeve from his grasp and kept running.

Dex joined Meyers at the door, and felt the few others in the room migrating over to join them. "Should we go see what's happening?" she asked.

Meyers shook his head firmly. "No, it's not worth the risk. We'll stay here and try to get updates from the dome authorities." He turned and pointed at a man nearby. "Get a connection to the administrator's office and keep at them until you know exactly what happened."

They returned to their desks, most moving listlessly as they tried to process this latest event. Dex couldn't help but think that the bomber was at work once more, most likely protecting Armstrong from any kind of attack from Aldrin.

It could also have been the Syndicate Marines, acting on orders from their commanders.

It took most of an hour for news to come in from the dome administrator's office across the square. Whatever had caused the explosion had been very close to the Aldrin entry point of the tunnel, and had been set off during a shift transfer at the guard post. Two full squads of Marines were presumed killed, as there had been no sign of survivors. The remaining squad had been pulled back, stationed around the administration building in case the bombing was a precursor to more attacks.

Meyers got a call late in the day, information being relayed that the Coalition frigates were aborting the effort to land Marines on Luna. They were leaving orbit to join with the rest of the fleet as they advanced to meet the Syndicate ships that were approaching from Mars. With Aldrin cut off from Armstrong, any attempt to storm the Syndicate dome was no longer viable.

The Guildhall emptied quickly as Meyers sent everyone home for the day, trying to maintain a positive demeanor until it was just he and Dex left. "I'm not going to let them abandon us," Meyers vowed. "We have five freighters that didn't get armed, correct? Make arrangements with those captains and our Earth contacts. I want supplies and people brought in. If the Coalition won't dedicate Marines to guard the dock repairs, then we'll arm our own people to ensure the work gets done. Perhaps it's time the Guild took a larger role, at least on Luna."

Dex spent the rest of the evening sending messages, talking with multiple people at a time on video calls, and getting everything organized to begin the operation. The most difficult part would be getting the first wave of people and supplies from a ship and into the dome, so she also worked with the head of the crew doing the docking facility repairs to arrange an entry point so newcomers wouldn't have to stay in pressure suits for very long.

The next morning, only three other people showed up at the Guildhall. The latest attack had driven the rest to remain holed up in their homes. The remaining squad of Marines maintained a perimeter around the administrative building across the square, moving into the building from the barracks that had been damaged by the explosion in the tunnel.

People started to line the square, calling out for news and asking why the Marines had abandoned the rest of the dome. It was a quiet protest at first, but by late afternoon the crowd had grown and the cries for answers had become angry and insistent.

Dex and Meyers stood in the doorway watching as the lights of the dome faded into false twilight. "This is what they want," the president said quietly. "Everyone keeps asking why the Syndicate ships would go weeks out of the way to Mars instead of heading straight for Earth. It's because they wanted to cause chaos like this. Give a gentle push to start the dominos falling, and people will start tearing things apart on their own and doing the work for them. Then the Syndicate can step in and claim to be restoring order and saving us from ourselves."

"This is why the cold war went on for so long," Dex said with a shrug. "The Coalition and Syndicate were both teetering on the edge of a cliff. One of them finally decided to push the other off, forgetting that it would send both crashing down. I'm sure scenes like this one are happening all over Earth, not just in Coalition territory."

Meyers grunted in agreement, and they watched the growing numbers and ferocity of the crowd as lamps around the square activated to provide a soft orange glow. The Marines facing the square had stoic expressions, worry evident in the way they glanced across at each other and darted into the building when the shift changed. Dex didn't know what would happen over the next few days, but she had little doubt that the Guild would receive the appreciation of Aldrin's citizens when they brought in their own armed guards.

Twenty Two

Her head was pounding when she woke, a steady thrum that seemed to pulse behind her eyes and felt powerful enough that she felt sure her head was expanding with each one. Groaning, she raised a hand to her head only to find that her wrists and forearms were tethered to a metal bar at her side. Opening her eyes, she was blinded in the bright white light above her. Tuya had to slit her eyes until they adjusted to the light and she could see well enough to open them wider.

Four separate restraints were attached to each arm, six on each leg, with two heavy straps wrapped around her stomach and chest. Tuya craned her head to look at her surroundings. She could see no one in the starkly white room. Two rolling trays were at the side of the bed, gleaming instruments with sharp edges arrayed on white linen. She felt a flutter of nerves in the pit of her stomach, and started to struggle against the restraints in search of weaknesses.

"There's no use in that," a high feminine voice said over speakers in the ceiling. "Those restraints are the strongest we have, and even your implants won't let you break through them."

"Where am I?" Tuya shouted hoarsely, her mouth parched.

"Surgical suite five," the voice replied. "We'll begin the procedure soon. You shouldn't be awake."

“Procedure?” Tuya went still and felt her body tingle as realization set in. They were going to remove her implants! When she suffered through the half-dozen backroom operations to have them installed, the doctors had cautioned her in advance about the side effects of removal. For six years her body had built itself around the implants, her strength coming from the cybernetic parts instead of increased muscle mass. After so long, removal of the implants would leave her body debilitated and unable to support itself. She would be almost paralyzed, and it would take months of painful effort to build herself back up again.

A door slid open and a nurse wrapped in a soft blue gown entered, holding a large needle. Tuya pulled against the restraints, trying to kick out a leg or throw an arm to disrupt the nurse, but they were too strong and tight. The bed didn’t even wobble beneath her as the needle was jabbed into her thigh and she felt the cold solution spread through her veins. Within minutes, she felt drowsy and dopey, and the room began to grow fuzzy in her vision.

“No,” she moaned, tears falling from the corner of her eyes.

The last thing she heard was the disembodied voice. “Relax, Miss Sansar. When you wake again, we’ll have those filthy implants removed and your body will be restored to its natural state.”

After almost two weeks in the stark white room, Tuya was finally deemed safe to be moved. The surgery to remove her implants had gone without a hitch, and the surgeon expressed satisfaction when he stopped in the next day to check the quickly healing cuts that covered her body. Tuya had been unable to do anything but lay limply on the table, tears in her eyes, as a nurse rolled her one way and then another so the surgeon could check the sutures on her back. From the moment she had regained consciousness, she'd been able to do no more than twitch a finger or toe after agonizing minutes of straining and focusing all her effort on the individual muscles.

The straps on the bed were left hanging, mute testimony to the fact that she no longer presented any threat at all as she was pushed through busy corridors toward whatever forgotten hole they planned to toss her next. Most of the people passing the bed didn't even bother to look at her, but the few who did often had cruel smiles. The word of her capture had spread quickly, along with the details of her cybernetic implants. The nurses who checked on her several times a day refused to speak a word to her, but would often hold conversations between themselves as if she were no more than furniture. Through them, she learned of the assault on Mars and the killing of all Coalition citizens on Deimos. She also felt a brief joy when she heard the news of the battle over Earth, though that was quickly overwhelmed by the sadness of the bombing on Luna. Knowing that five freighters had been destroyed in the blasts, she couldn't help but think of her friends on the *Vagabond* and wonder if they'd been there.

Tuya started to recognize the corridors they were passing through after fifteen minutes of travel, and felt her heart drop and soar at the same time. This was the way to the holding cells where her brother had been held for three months now, and she started to wonder if she might be put into the same cell with him. The bed rolled to a stop, and a familiar figure appeared above her. The sharp features and brown hair would forever be imprinted upon her memory, the face of the man who had brought so much misery and pain into her life.

"Miss Sansar," Davis said, his eyes roaming across her body, covered by a thin white sheet. "I'm truly sorry that things had to reach this point, but you should have escaped with the others when you had the chance."

Feeling moisture slide down from the corner of an eye, Tuya tried to work up her old passionate rage. The most she could manage was a dull aching sense of loss. "I hope you burn for this," she said tonelessly. "I hope this ship is destroyed, and I hope that every one of you evil bastards feels every millisecond of the pain as you die."

"I can appreciate why you would feel that way, but we are only putting the system back into rightful order. It's unnatural for two powerful entities to constantly be holding each other back from advancing. Humanity was built by constant forward progress, and it's time for that to begin again."

She turned a furrowed gaze to his face. "You really believe that, don't you? Killing thousands of innocent people, maybe even millions by the time this is all done, is nothing to you so long as what you feel is right prevails over what they feel is right."

“This is not about right or wrong, Miss Sansar. It is about what should be.” Davis looked up, turning his attention down the corridor to where she remembered the Marine standing guard outside the holding cells corridor. “This war will be over in a matter of weeks, I assure you. The Coalition fleet is already advancing to meet us, and that confrontation is a week away.” He returned his eyes to meet hers, and then turned sharply and walked away down the corridor.

The bed was pushed forward again, a wheel squeaking insistently in protest as they continued down the corridor for several hundred yards. “Prisoner 97A3,” one of the nurses stated, and the Marine bent to look at her as he held a tablet to get a scan of her face and biometric data.

“Room four,” the Marine said when the process was done, and the bed was pushed forward again. Tuya heard a door hiss open as the bed made a sharp turn to enter a room with steel gray walls and ceiling. Turning her head, she could see a bunk against the wall with thin bedding that would provide only minimal protection during acceleration and braking burns. There was a bare toilet and sink against the opposite wall, with no mirrors in the room at all.

The nurses grunted as they lifted the sheet she was lying on, and transferred her to the bunk. They didn't bother zipping her into the protective bedding, just laid her on top of the bunk and wheeled the gurney out of the room. Tuya was left in silence after the door closed, wondering how long she would last in her current state. She couldn't feed herself, couldn't clean herself, couldn't even scratch the itch on her nose that had been driving her crazy for the last half hour.

The silence stretched out for what seemed hours but could have been seconds. Her mind was drifting, her eyes staring into space, and she felt totally disconnected from reality.

It was a small sound that brought her back, a sound that made her think of claws scratching against metal. Blinking, she focused on the sound and turned her head to where a small vent sat low in the wall on the other side of the room. The scratching stopped, and a kind of quiet moaning sound came from the vent for several seconds before stopping and then starting again. The scratching started again, followed by the moaning, a pattern that repeated for half an hour before stopping.

Tuya had been staring at the wall throughout the strange occurrence, and it took her brain a long time to process the sounds and realize that she was hearing a voice. It had been pitched low, just above a whisper, a sound that she couldn't possibly make out from where she was. Then she realized that it had to be someone in the cell next to hers trying to talk to the new prisoner, and hope flared as she thought of Altan. Could it be her brother, separated from her by a single bulkhead?

There was only one way she was going to find out. She would have to build her strength enough to move her body across the room to be closer to the vent. It would take days, if not weeks, but she had a new purpose to drive her. If she let herself wither away and die, then the Syndicate would win and she would go into whatever afterlife might exist with a shameful mark against her.

For the first time in weeks, she felt her mouth twisting with anger as she strained to move her muscles. She focused on them one at a time, moving first her fingers and then her wrists and then clenching her biceps. The process took hours to go through her entire body, and she was soaked with perspiration and breathing heavily with pain at the end. But she felt good at the same time, felt the anger and determination fueling her again. After resting for a minute, she started the process all over again.

Tuya could count the days only by counting the number of times she was fed. The first day, a nurse hooked up an IV with a bag of clear fluids. He set a cup of steaming broth near her mouth, allowing her to sip from a straw as he looked over her sutures. A Marine had followed the nurse in, standing beside the door and watching as her naked body was revealed when the sheet was tossed aside. She couldn't see the Marine, but could imagine the leer that would undoubtedly be on his face. Her breasts were one of the few parts of her body not slashed open in the surgery and covered with pink healing scars.

"It all looks good," the nurse pronounced as he tugged the sheet up to drape across her legs where it served no purpose. He pulled away the half-full bag of fluids and vitamins her body needed, picked up the mostly empty cup of broth, and looked at her in disgust. Her bladder had emptied on the bunk an hour before, no arrangements made for her inability to get to the toilet several feet away. "I won't need to come back, the sutures will naturally degrade and fade away."

"I'm not feeding her," the Marine said, waving a hand at the broth and straw.

The nurse shrugged as he walked away from the bed. "That's not my concern. Leave a tray. If she wants to eat she'll have to figure it out on her own."

Since that visit, a tray had been set on the table near the bunk twice a day. She knew it was morning and evening because the Marines were different each time. The first one would always wish her a cheery good morning as she set the tray on the table and walked out of the room. Five times she'd heard the chipper tones, and four times heard the complaining grumble of the evening Marine who always blamed her for not eating the food.

She smiled in anticipation of his next visit as the door opened and the Marine walked in to drop the tray on the table with a clatter. His face came into view as he bent to look down at her still exposed and emaciated body. He leered at her, winked with a nasty smile, and then was gone as the door hissed closed behind him.

They sent someone in to sanitize the room when the smell of urine on the bunk got too bad, and the one time her bowels voided. Each time she was moved back onto the thin bed, the blanket was tossed across her legs or left to fall to the floor.

Tuya grunted, teeth bared as she strained with the effort, and managed to move her left arm up to where she could push against the short lip of the bunk. Her torso slid on the smooth fabric of the zippered bed, and she hit the wall after several inches. Breathing hard, she paused to gather her strength and then pushed again and worked to lift her head and back high enough that she started to slide up the wall. Finally lying in a roughly upright position, she could see the brown slop on the tray. Her mouth watered at the sight, and her stomach began to rumble and complain. Five days without food would have been torture before she realized what torture really was. It was only the kindness of the morning Marine giving her sips of water that had kept her body going at all.

With supreme effort, she raised the hand closest to the table. Her arm was shaking as it rose, and there were moments that she felt sure that she would not get it high enough. Finally, her hand was resting on the table. Her determination had gotten her farther than she would ever have expected when she thought about the implants being removed, and she started to wonder if the drawbacks had been overstated. It could also be that she had relied on her implants much less than most people who took the risk of getting them, working hard to use normal strength whenever possible.

Sliding her hand along the table, she was able to hook a couple of fingers over the side of the tray and slowly pull it closer. She stared at the mushy pile that offered nutrition and not much else, tongue darting out to lick her lips as she wrapped her hand around the plastic spoon sticking out of the food. It took all of her concentration to hold the spoon steady with the small amount of food it contained as she brought it to her lips with slow jerky movements. Seeing the spoon beginning to tilt as it got closer, she darted her head forward to snap her teeth over the utensil. Eyes closed in ecstasy, she sucked the spoon dry and swallowed the tasteless brown mush.

The Marine guard would be returning soon to retrieve the tray, so Tuya knew that she had to move as quickly as her pain-wracked body and rebuilding muscles would allow. While reaching over for a second small spoonful, she was pushing at the bed with her other hand to slide her body closer to the table that the tray rested on. After a second bite, her eyes moved to the small cup of liquid resting on the tray with a straw tilted over the edge. Leaning in to get her lips closer to the straw, she misjudged her abdominal strength and flopped down to hit the table with a shoulder.

Grunting with pain, she watched the cup wobble and start to fall. It was an extreme stroke of luck that sent the cup in her direction, dropping just enough to lean against the tall edge of the tray. A bit of the green liquid splashed out to land on the table and Tuya's cheek, but the straw was now close enough that she could clamp her mouth over it and greedily suck up what proved to be some kind of vegetable puree mixed with copious amounts of water.

When the door of the cell hissed open several minutes later, she had managed to force herself upright once more. A wicked smile met the Marine as he stopped in shock just inside the door, surprised at seeing her moved from the position she had occupied the last five days. She had managed only half a dozen bites of the mushy food, but the cup was drained as much as it could be in its awkward position.

The Marine grunted and frowned, stepping forward almost angrily to grab the tray and pull it away. "I guess you can start cleaning yourself up now, if you're so improved. This room better be spotless tomorrow, or you'll get the same punishments as the other prisoners." He walked out of the room only to return moments later to toss a plastic parcel on the floor. "Get in your jumpsuit, prisoner. You get punished for tearing or staining that, too." He grinned maliciously as he turned and left the cell again.

Tuya felt her own smile fade as she turned tired eyes to look at the package on the floor. She knew it would take at least an hour to get herself down to reach it, open it, and then somehow get herself into the jumpsuit. The prospect of covering her nakedness was extremely appealing, however, and it would also get her closer to the vent on the far wall.

The guard had mentioned another prisoner, his words making it almost certain that the noises from the vent had to be from her brother in the next cell. The sounds had repeated for several days, but then stopped. She could only hope that she would be able to make enough noise to get Altan's attention without alerting the guards.

Her legs proved somewhat steadier than her arms had been, wobbling as she slid off the bunk but supporting most of her weight when she dropped to her knees. Leaning forward to place her palms on the ground she rocked herself forward until she was able to swing an arm out and gain a few inches. Repeating the process over and over again, she crawled across the cold steel floor.

The pain of her overtaxed rebuilding muscles drowned out the discomfort from her palms and knees, but she was ecstatic when she reached the plastic parcel and was able to open it with little effort. The white jumpsuit slid out to the floor, and her luck held as she saw that the zippers were already open. She would just have to slide her arms and legs in and then pull it closed in front and pull the zipper up. Easy, right?

Sweating, straining, and swearing, she managed to get herself dressed in under half an hour and lay back on the hard floor to smile up at the ceiling in victory. The bastards may have taken her strength, but no one could take away her determination and anger. It had taken her too long to realize that, but now she finally started to feel more in control of her life again, even if it was just the ability to eat and clean herself.

Rolling was easier now that she was already on the floor, and it only took a few shoves to get herself the rest of the way across the small cell so that she lay by the tiny vent. It had looked small from the bed, but looked even smaller when she was next to it. No more than a couple of inches square with half a dozen slits for air intake or output, it was almost at her mouth level as she lay with her head flat on the floor.

"Hello?" she called quietly. "Are you there?" Tuya waited, then repeated the calls over and over. After a while, she managed to lift an arm and run her long ragged nails down the wall creating a scratching sound that was very similar to what she had heard days before.

After ten minutes, she was on the verge of giving up when she heard a faint reply. "I'm here," she thought the voice said. There was an echoing quality to it that made it difficult to distinguish each word.

"Who are you?" she asked, slowly and deliberately to be heard better through the echoes.

“No names!” the voice cried quietly, and she felt sure it was a male voice. Her heart soared and she was about to ask if he was Altan when the next sentence stopped her. “The guards don’t like it if we know names. They are very nasty guards.”

“Very well,” she replied after a pause. “How long have you been here?”

“I don’t know. Weeks, maybe months. It’s hard to keep track of the days.”

“How many food trays have you received? Two a day, remember.”

A chuckle could be heard faintly from the other side. “That’s what they want you to believe. I counted between them, and some come within a few hours while others are half a day or more. You could be receiving two trays one day, and four the next, never realizing.”

Tuya was stunned, and tried to think back and see if it was possible. She’d been so intent on building her muscles back up to get to this point that she could have passed an entire day between trays without realizing it. It dawned on her how easy it was to lose track of time when there was no reference. When she slept, was it for thirty minutes or twelve hours? There was no way to tell since she always felt tired from the effort of her exercises, and the boredom of having nothing else to focus her attention on.

The voice interrupted her thoughts. “Do you want to get out of here? I have a plan, a good plan, but it’ll take two of us.”

TWENTY THREE

"We're only days out from meeting the Coalition fleet," Davis said, standing in front of his assault team in the briefing room. "You've all been training for this fight, you've run the scenarios a hundred times at least. I know that you're ready." The squad shouted approval, smiling and happy for what they knew would come.

"The admiral has ordered Ghost Squad to infiltrate and disable the lead frigate, called *Waterloo*. I have told him that this is a mission we can easily accomplish, a mission that a team like ours was built for. I've also told him that my goal is not disabling, but taking control of the Coalition frigate." He gestured, and the room went dark as a holographic representation of the enemy ship appeared between him and the seated squad. "We will board the insertion pods at fifteen hundred hours, and be fired from the torpedo tubes to achieve maximum velocity. This keeps us from having to use thrusters that could be detected by their long-range sensors. Based on current speeds and projected flight paths, we should all make contact with the *Waterloo* in thirty-nine and a half hours."

Davis pulled the image around, expanding it so everyone could see a small area of the ship that he circled with a finger. "This is one of their maintenance airlocks. Our pods will fire braking thrusters for no more than five seconds before making impact with the hull of the ship. All nine insertion pods will be computer controlled to make contact at the same moment, firing grappling hooks into the hull plating to secure the pods tightly to the skin of the frigate. This section has a large blind spot, where their sensors can't get a reading within several meters of the hull, but our landing will still create enough noise that I would expect someone will be sent out to check the area. We'll have three minutes to exit the pods, gather weapons and gear, and circle the airlock to be ready for whoever exits. Any questions so far?"

He looked around the room and saw nothing but rapt attention from his soldiers. "Once inside the ship, we divide into two groups. Group One will be with me, targeting the bridge of the frigate in our attempt to gain control of the ship. The goal is to do so without allowing them to send out warnings of a boarding, so that we can turn the ship's weapons on the unsuspecting fleet and do as much damage as possible in the early stages of the battle, before the *Indomitable* arrives.

"Group Two will head for Engineering. Once there, explosives will be placed so as to disable the ship in the event that One is unable to succeed in their mission. Should enemy forces prevent extraction from the ship, Two will also ensure that they carry enough explosives to trigger a reactor meltdown and destroy the ship entirely. An explosion of the frigate's reactor will create a debris field large enough to severely damage and possible destroy any other ships nearby."

Davis paused, his eyes traveling around the room. "Now, as you all know one of our pods was used to intercept the freighter in the asteroid belt and return it to the *Indomitable*. That insertion pod was still on the freighter when the crew effected their escape, and is therefore lost to us. Someone will have to be left behind, and won't be able to participate in the mission. Is there anyone who would like to volunteer to remain on the *Indomitable*?" He let the silence stretch out for several minutes, maintaining a neutral expression as he waited to see if anyone would prove to have less than the desired zeal for the mission. None of the squad so much as looked to be flirting with the idea of raising their hand.

"Excellent. I knew that we trained the best of the best. You leave the decision in my hands, and I assure you that whatever choice I make is not a reflection on your skills. Dismissed. Meet back here at fourteen hundred hours for final mission prep."

The eight members of Ghost Squad filed from the room, Anders and Davis left behind. The sergeant was seated with one leg stretched out in front of him, hands folded over his stomach as he looked at his lieutenant. "How in the hell do you decide which of them to leave back, sir? This may be the best team I've worked with in all my years as a Marine."

"It's not an easy decision. I have to admit that I asked one of the ensigns in Engineering about the possibility of modifying a pod to allow for two passengers, but the work required would have taken a week and required materials not available on the ship."

"The only good thing is that our team is trained to be proficient in multiple fields, sir. Leaving someone behind isn't taking away a skillset that could be needed down the line. Though an extra gun will be missed if we get into a firefight with the Marines on the frigate."

"Let's hope that we're able to avoid such an eventuality. Our men and women may be trained for all manner of combat situations, but even the best squad is hard pressed to win a battle against five or six times their number."

"You realize that maintenance airlock is far from the bridge, sir? Main Engineering section is only a few corridors away, but you're going to be very exposed traveling through half the frigate to approach the bridge."

Davis smiled tightly. "I have an idea of how to improve our odds there. Go get some rest while you can, sergeant. I want you back here at thirteen hundred so we can lock down the final details before the rest of the squad arrives."

When Anders returned to the briefing room, he chuckled at finding Davis still looking over the hologram of the Coalition frigate. "Did you even step outside the room in the last few hours, sir?"

"Too much to do, sergeant, as always. I have made a decision, however, and I'm glad you're here." Davis turned to look somberly at the sergeant who had been assigned to work with him a little more than a year before, when the admiral approved the plan to form the assault team. The two men had worked together well, forming a bond of friendship that made it hard for him to say the next words.

"Sergeant Anders, I have selected you to remain behind on *Indomitable*. Should something happen to myself and the rest of the team, I'll die knowing that you're here to build a new team just as good as Ghost Squad. If not better."

Anders looked at him, stricken with the words. "But, sir, you need me to lead the Group Two. To lead them into Engineering and destroy the frigate if the bridge can't be taken."

"The admiral has approved the promotion for Corporal Lopez. She will lead Group Two in your place." Davis gripped the sergeant's arm. "It was not an easy decision to make, but I feel it's the right one. Our odds of succeeding on this mission are low, as you know. Having you here to build another Ghost Squad if the worst happens, or to lead the remnants of the team should they manage to leave the frigate without me, will allow me to focus on the mission."

Anders couldn't meet his gaze, looking away as his mouth worked to form words. Finally, he nodded bleakly and stumbled to sit in one of the chairs. "I don't like being left behind, sir, but I understand your reasoning. Have you let Lopez know yet?"

"She knows about the promotion being granted, the rest she'll learn with the others when the final briefing begins."

The two men passed the rest of the hour in silence, each lost in their thoughts as they waited for the assault team to enter and fill the seats. They hooted with delight at the news that Lopez would lead Group Two, but grumbled when they learned that Anders would remain on the cruiser. At the same time, Davis could see relief in the eyes of every soldier to learn that they weren't the one selected.

When he dismissed the squad to go climb into their insertion pods, he stiffened and saluted the sergeant. Every member of the team joined him, and Anders stared at them for a few moments before standing to return the salute. "Good luck, Ghost Squad," he told them as they left.

It took most of an hour to get the insertion pods packed with gear and the soldiers, buttoned up tight, and then loaded in the torpedo tubes. The electromagnetic firing system would shoot the pods from the tubes at a force equivalent to more than twenty G's, generating enough speed to cross the distance between the rapidly converging fleets and arrive six hours before the Syndicate ships could. It was a process survivable only because of the special gel that could fill the pods to suspend each soldier in a state where they felt almost no motion or gravitational forces at all. They were also restricted to using verbal commands through their helmet HUDs to communicate with the pod's systems.

Davis watched as his group were loaded into the pods, knowing the same process would be happening in the second torpedo bay where Group Two had assembled. Four men and women he had spent the last year training, running through scenario after scenario as they learned the tactics and methods he believed would allow a small squad to fight against an entire ship. Now, they would finally get to test themselves and find out if he was right.

He stepped into his pod, and lowered himself to lie in the gel that already half filled it. The viscous blue liquid seeped around the matte black armor and helmet, encasing him protectively. He felt the lid of the pod close, the locks engage, and then the pod being rolled into the chamber of the torpedo launcher. There was silence within the pod, the only sounds his breath and the blood pounding through his body. Minutes stretched out as he waited, knowing that the pods would all be fired at the exact same moment to ensure they arrived at the target landing zone simultaneously. Davis could feel his mind starting to wander when he felt a small jerk and knew that his pod had just been ejected from the *Indomitable* at an incredible speed. He settled in for the long trip through space, his only company the thoughts in his head and the occasional updates from the extremely low-powered sensors of the pod.

A repeating tone woke him from a deep sleep, the sound alerting him that they were ten minutes out from impact with the *Waterloo*. Davis cast his eyes across the screen of his HUD, verifying the rest of the team were exactly where they should be. He felt himself tensing up in anticipation of the intercept landing on the hull of the frigate, feeling the thrill of the action to come after so long spent in training and supervisory duties. If not for the time he rode a pod to intercept the freighter, he would have forgotten this thrill months ago.

The braking thrusters fired right on time, the brief burst sufficient to slow the pod so that it could fire six barbed titanium hooks into the hull of the ship it was passing over. The strong tethers pulled tight, bringing the pod to an immediate stop relative to the velocity of the frigate itself, and then reeled it in until the pod settled mere inches off the hull. The gel drained away into special reservoirs within seconds, and the lid popped open with a hiss of air.

Davis jumped to his feet, grabbed a small bag that he slung over his shoulders, and rushed to take position around the airlock. Within thirty seconds of making contact with the frigate, Ghost Squad was assembled and waiting. One of the soldiers edged a small camera stalk forward to get a view though the small, thick window in the airlock door. "No movement," he reported over the squad's comms, a tight beam system that couldn't be intercepted and wouldn't register on the Coalition systems.

"Patch into the controls," Davis ordered. Another soldier edged forward to open a small hatch and access the emergency entry/exit panel. She plugged two leads from her suit computer into the panel and started a program that worked to break the extremely strong military encryption. It took twenty seconds for her to report that the panel was in her control. After ensuring that there was still no movement from within, he gave the order to open the airlock.

The door irised open, and Group Two dropped in one by one with Corporal Lopez taking the rear. The airlock was closed and then the inner door opened, so the soldiers could spill out into the antechamber. They took up positions to guard against anyone sent to investigate the noise of their landing.

"It looks like they either didn't hear the noise or aren't very curious, sir," Lopez said over the comms as they all crouched out of view from anyone in the corridor.

“Get your team close to Engineering, Corporal. Use the recon drones, and make sure you’re not seen.” The small drones were tiny nano-engineered cameras that could fly as far as three hundred meters away from the control set carried by one soldier in each group. It was yet another extremely expensive bit of gear his assault team carried that would never be allowed into the hands of normal Marines.

Davis turned to the soldiers of Group One, giving the hand signal to advance. The assault suits contained small magnets in the boots that could keep them anchored to the hull of a ship, but were only a tenth as powerful as normal mag boots. That made it much easier to miss a step and be lost to drift away into space. They eschewed the tether rails as they glided across the frigate’s hull, moving in a direct line for their target location. Lopez sent constant updates, the signal growing fainter and more scratchy with distance and interference. Group Two had holed up in a small room not far from the main Engineering section by the time One reached their destination.

Comparing the map of the ship to their location, he verified they were over the right spot. This was a small hump in the hull, a place where the sensors and communication equipment met in a jumble of relays and switches. These were spread all over the frigate, in almost the same position they occupied on Syndicate frigates, and this one was very near the bridge of the ship. Two of the soldiers carried small laser cutting tools, which they used to slice small sections of hull away until there was enough room for each of them to enter the void between the inner and outer hull.

Wriggling into the tight space, Davis watched with satisfaction as the last soldier to drop in pulled the cut-out sections into place and touched the laser torch to the seams to weld them lightly together. It had taken only thirty seconds to complete the entry, minimizing the chance of alarms about the loss of lightly pressurized air between the hulls.

Once the pressure in the space between the hulls had equalized, they pierced the inner hull and dropped a small camera through the hole to get a view of the room below them. The captain's quarters were adjacent to the bridge, the perfect entry point for Davis's group. They could be almost certain the Fleet Admiral, occupying the quarters while on board, would be on the bridge or elsewhere in the ship with the Syndicate fleet so close to intercept. His assumption was proved correct, the room unoccupied and ready for them to drop in.

Another small entry point was cut through the inner hull, a single piece this time so that it could be easily pulled away and then welded back into place. Once they were inside the ship, there would be no need to use the holes as an exit. The assault squad would either succeed in their mission or go down fighting, taking as many of the enemy with them as they possibly could.

Davis dropped into the quarters, landing silently and stepping quickly toward the door to focus his suit sensors on any sounds from outside. Nothing was picked up, and by the time the rest of the team was behind him with the entry point crudely reattached he was ready to signal the advance. "Stay tight," he reminded the four soldiers with him. "When we enter the bridge, take out the Marines first. Containment of the room is second, prevent anyone going in or out. Third goal is prevent any communication with the rest of the frigate or the fleet. Once that's done, we force whatever command staff is present to give their access codes. If we have to kill them to do so, we will."

He waited for any questions, and then waved one of the soldiers forward to take point as a small map of the bridge appeared on all of their HUDs. If all went well, Ghost Squad would have control of the frigate's bridge within less than a minute and be ready to spring a trap against the other Coalition ships before the battle began.

TWENTY FOUR

Ensign Natalia Avila. It still sounded wrong every time one of the half dozen people that now reported to her said it. She always thought of childhood games, when she and her friends would pretend to be captains of starships. Except for the times she was waiting for someone to laugh and tell her it had all been one big joke as they pulled the rank pip from her chest. That never happened, though, and after two weeks she was feeling more comfortable with the title. She no longer had to be called several times before she realized people were talking to her.

Lieutenant Richtaus had been released from the medical bay just the day before, and tracked her down to wrap her in a tight hug that demonstrated proficiency with the prosthetic arm that had been grafted to her shoulder. "I always knew you'd be going places," Mags had said, beaming proudly. "Ensign."

Nat still reported to Mags, but now served as a conduit for the crew of her Engineering section. She would get her orders from the lieutenant, and then pass those orders on to the half dozen crew of her shift. Many of them had worked alongside her for a year or more, but none seemed to harbor any ill will for her sudden elevation to the officer ranks. She felt incredibly grateful for that, and felt it spurred her to excel at her new rank. There would be an officer candidate test waiting for her to take if the fleet survived the upcoming battle, and she was already working hard to study the materials in her off hours.

Starting her shift, Nat was glad to see Mags already hard at work. "It's good to have you back, lieutenant. You sure you want to jump back in the day before we meet the Syndicate fleet?"

"No time better," Mags insisted. "There's a lot of work to get done to make sure the ship is in top condition before we take on that *Indomitable* beast."

"Yes, ma'am." Nat saluted, fighting a giddy grin as she remembered how contemptuous she had been of the gesture when she had seen it as simple subservience. Now she saw it as a sign of respect for her superior officer, a respect that was returned and would be owed to her if she earned a promotion to higher ranks in the future.

The two women spent an hour going over reports from around the ship, and Mags looked through all the repair logs of the issues handled while she was stuck in the med bay. She nodded with satisfaction as she scanned the list. "You've done excellent work, ensign, just as I expected. I think you've even managed to achieve an efficiency level higher than the Chief could ever have dreamed."

"Thank you, ma'am. I had a wonderful officer who showed me how to be a good leader."

Chuckling, Mags set aside her tablet and leaned against the console they were using. "Flattery will get you everywhere, ensign. Especially when it's stone cold truth. Has the Chief talked to you about where you'll be stationed before and during the battle yet?"

Nat frowned and shook her head. "I assumed we would be handling any repair needs that came up. In a more organized manner than during the battle over Earth, hopefully."

"Yeah, don't get me started on that shit show. The *Waterloo* is expected to be in weapons range of the Syndicate ships by thirteen hundred tomorrow afternoon. You and your team will be stationed on the bridge starting at eleven hundred. The captain has been impressed with your work, and feels you'll be an asset to him there."

"That's quite an honor, one I'm not sure I deserve. Do you have any advice for me?"

"Yeah, Nat, don't screw up." Mags grinned. "Just do what you always do, and you'll be fine. I think the captain and admiral are expecting this to be a tough battle, anticipating a lot of damage inflicted on the *Waterloo* since we're in the vanguard. We're already more vulnerable after the rushed repairs of the damage sustained in the battle over Earth. Your team will be dedicated to keeping the bridge systems as functional as possible."

"We'll do our best, ma'am."

"I know you will, ensign. Now, gather your team and let's get today's work done. Looks like they have us running all over the ship with no rhyme or reason to it. Typical senior officers setting the schedule."

Janet was amused to learn they would both be stationed on the bridge during the battle. They'd shared a cabin for ten months, and this would be the first time their duties brought them together. It was all the more bittersweet with the knowledge that Nat would be moving into her own small cabin once the promotion was secured with a passing test score. Janet would have to learn how to live with a new roommate, while Nat would have to learn to live with no roommate at all.

Leaving the cabin that morning, Janet gave a mocking salute as they turned to go separate directions down the corridor. "I'll see you on the bridge, madam ensign." The formal nonsense of the title always caused both of them to giggle.

Nat entered her Engineering section to find the team already waiting, dressed in the cleanest and crispest jumpsuits and carrying diagnostic kits that had been cleaned and polished to a shine. She couldn't help but smile at the sight of them arrayed as if for a parade.

"I see we're all ready to invade the bridge and show those pampered idiots how to properly keep a ship running."

"Yes, ma'am," one crewman said proudly, his chest seeming to expand with pride.

"Did you test your kits, make sure everything is charged and every tool is accounted for?" The crew nodded, one of them pushing forward a kit that they had prepared for her to carry. "Okay, let's get up there and report for duty early."

The trip to the bridge was long, the corridors full of people scurrying from one place to another as the ship prepared for battle. Half a dozen fighter pilots trotted past at one point, fully suited up and carrying the emergency oxygen tanks they would use if they had to bail out of their attack craft during the battle. Nat and her team arrived at the bridge ten minutes before eleven hundred, to be greeted by a

Marine guard wholly unimpressed with their early arrival. After a bit of grumbling and checking ID cards, he let them enter.

In advance of the battle, the wedge-shaped bridge was the closest Nat had ever seen to controlled chaos. It seemed as if the person at every station was calling out status reports to the junior officers that stood behind them passing on the reports to senior officers. Above it all, the captain was standing near the command deck rail, where he could look over every station and see the large displays at the front and along the sides of the bridge that showed the view beyond the ship. Captain Andrews noticed the engineering crew enter, his eyes flicking over them before returning to the hive of activity.

"Two of you find a place up front, two in the middle, and two back here with me. Make sure you can see all the stations in your section and be ready to move fast if someone calls for assistance. Stay calm, keep your heads, and we'll all get through this." She patted each of them on the shoulder as they passed to split up and find places to station themselves. A touch on her sleeve startled her, and she turned to find a crewman waiting just behind her.

"The captain would like to see you, ensign." She nodded and followed the man up a curving stair to the command deck. A curved section was set up at the back with half a dozen stations for officers to use as needed to monitor the activity below, with only one of the seats currently occupied. The captain was still standing at the rail, and she approached and held a salute until he turned to return the gesture and then waved her into a relaxed stance.

“Welcome to the bridge, ensign. Let’s hope things go as well as they did the last time you were here.” He paused and looked over his shoulder as one of the crew called out in a shrill voice, but turned back when it appeared to not be an urgent issue. “I’d like you to take one of the stations here for the duration. You’ll have access to all of our status reports to manage your team’s work for best effect.”

“It would be an honor, sir.” Nat couldn’t believe she’d been invited to be on the command deck during the battle. She saw Janet staring up at her from the middle of the bridge below, eyebrows raised above a sardonic grin. Turning away, she took a seat at an empty station and immediately connected to the channel her team used. She checked in with each of them, letting them know she had access to the status reports and might divert their attention if needed during their shift on the bridge.

She kept one ear tuned to the conversations around her as she worked, listening to the ensign talking with the officers on the bridge below to verify data that was streaming in. The captain was quiet, and she heard only a murmured greeting as the admiral entered the command deck to join him at the rail. His aides followed behind, taking spots at the bank of stations.

“All frigates are reporting as ready, and all weapons hot,” an ensign called out from another station. Nat thought that he must be monitoring communications, since she knew the woman who had just taken a seat next to her would be in charge of the *Waterloo*’s weapons and defenses. She could see the displays that showed green status indicators for all the railguns, torpedo tubes, and smaller defensive guns.

Another indicator seemed to display the hull integrity and looked to be broken into several dozen chunks to show the different parts of the frigate.

At noon, a small cart was rolled onto the command deck by a purser. Nat was amazed to see plates of quartered sandwiches, fruits from the ship's hydroponics, and a steaming pot of coffee. The captain and admiral made small plates for their lunch, and the commander sitting next to Nat nudged her. "Come get some chow. Going into a battle on an empty stomach does no one any good." She followed the woman to the tray, finding the sandwiches filled with meat paste that tasted like turkey and ham. The bread was freshly baked for the officer's mess, and she resolved to visit the wardroom for meals going forward instead of using the main galley.

On the bridge below, she saw protein bars being handed out so the crew could eat at their stations. The displays showed the rapidly approaching Syndicate fleet, the *Indomitable* so large that it dwarfed the six frigates traveling in formation around it, making them appear insignificant. She knew both fleets were already firing their braking thrusters. The first salvoes would be fired as the ships passed each other to then flip and burn hard to reverse momentum and approach the enemy again.

Once her meal was completed, Nat returned to her station and checked in with the team below to make sure they filled their stomachs as well. They all checked in and complained only of boredom as they had nothing to do but watch the bridge crew work. "In another hour, you'll be wishing you could go back to being bored," she told them.

She knew the sight of the Syndicate ships on the massive displays was causing them to feel the same nervousness that she did.

"Prepare fighters for launch," the admiral spoke from the rail. The communications ensign acknowledged and then started to pass the order through the fleet. Nat could picture the docking bay as the small craft were pulled down from storage racks and niches to be placed on the floor of the bay so maintenance crews could swarm over them and ensure that all systems were functioning properly.

It seemed too soon when the admiral ordered a five-minute countdown for the fighters to be launched from all frigates at the same moment. The thrust of their engines combined with the forward momentum from the frigates would catapult them forward to begin strafing and bombing runs against the enemy ships. The pilots would attempt to disable as many railguns or defensive emplacements as they could to give the Coalition ships an advantage over their foes.

"Fighters launching," the communications officer called out. Nat heard the door beside her station hiss open. She turned and gasped. Two matte black armored soldiers rushed onto the command deck. They swung their rifles to point at the waiting officers. Below, she heard the faint huffing sound of a rifle firing. More intruders must have entered the main bridge. Within seconds the sounds of fighting ceased and a harshly modulated voice called up an all clear.

A third soldier strode through the open door, waving to lock down the entry point in passing, and stopped in front of the captain and admiral. The voice that emitted from the helmet speakers was heavily modified. The distortion prevented Nat from knowing if the person inside the armor was male or female, and the armor itself was fitted in such a way that it was impossible to determine gender from the body shape.

"Fleet Admiral Holgerson, Captain Andrews." The enemy soldier bowed his head slightly as he spoke each name. "The Syndicate is now in control of your bridge, and I have soldiers taking control in other sections of the ship, as well. You will provide me with your access codes to the ship's systems."

Nat looked at the station next to her, surprised to see that the commander there had locked the station. She knew it must be something covered in the training that officers received, something she hadn't yet gone through. Eyes darting around at the enemy soldiers, she felt certain their attention was on the captain and admiral. She moved her hand slowly to type a few words on the terminal and then hit the button that locked down the station so that only her codes or those of the captain or admiral could render it useful again.

The Fleet Admiral raised his head in a display of haughty contempt. "There is no way you could sneak enough troops aboard a ship like the *Waterloo* to take control of all the important sections. Whoever you are, I will accept your surrender and ensure you are treated well until the end of hostilities between our two governments if you lay down your weapons."

The soldier who was obviously in charge of the invaders raised two fingers, and one of the soldiers turned to fire their rifle. It had taken less than a second, and Nat was shocked to see blood blooming across the uniform tunic of the communications ensign. The man looked down at his chest in surprise, raising a hand to touch his uniform even as he slumped out of the chair and crumpled to the floor.

"You will give me your codes, or I will kill each member of your command staff one by one," the lead soldier informed them in the grating voice.

Captain Andrews grimaced as he looked at the dead ensign, jaw clenching tightly. "We will not give in to your demands. Marines will be on the way now to retake the bridge, and then we'll see how you like watching your own people die."

Fingers were raised again, and with a quick turn the commander sitting next to Nat was shot in the same spot on her chest, the round piercing her heart with deadly accuracy. A bit of blood splashed across Nat's cheek, and she let out a yelp of shock. The woman next to her snarled and started to push herself up to rush the soldier who shot her. She took two halting steps before crumpling to the deck.

"Your Marines will find it hard to get past doors that have been locked down," the lead enemy soldier said. "I can do this all afternoon, captain. You will give me the codes and turn the *Waterloo* over to my control, or we will stand here in a sea of blood from your dead crew as the Syndicate fleet destroys this ship around you."

Neither the admiral nor the captain replied. They stood in stoic silence as fingers were raised yet again and a shot killed the second of the admiral's aides. Nat was the last remaining junior officer at the bank of terminals. She could feel her heart beating a thousand miles a minute.

Amazingly, a veil of calmness seemed to descend upon her and she faced the prospect with clear thinking. She knew the admiral would never break, but could see the captain losing his resolution as he continued watching people die around him. A thought blazed in her head, and she didn't take time to consider it before turning to quickly type in her unlock code and then send a series of commands to the ship's computer.

One of the soldiers in matte black had seen her turn. He swung his rifle around and barked at her to stop. She ignored him as she typed furiously, fingers flying across the keyboard and tapping buttons on the terminal as they came up to initiate the commands. "Desist or you *will* be shot," the leader of the enemy troops barked, but she ignored him as well. She knew that her time was short no matter what happened. It was a minor miracle that they hadn't shot her already.

From the corner of her eye she saw a rifle raised to point at her head, the movement so slow in her perception that it was like watching someone wade through water. She typed in the last command, pressed the button to lock down her station, and swiveled to face the barrel of the rifle. On the bridge below, several of the crew called out in shock as the ship shuddered and seemed to jump forward.

“What did you do?” the enemy leader demanded, striding across the deck to grab her tightly by the arm and lift her from the chair. She could feel his grip crushing her upper arm. “What did you do?” he asked again.

Nat only smiled serenely, satisfied that at the very least she had spoiled whatever plans these Syndicate soldiers had in mind for the *Waterloo*. A hand swung up and cracked against her jaw, throwing her head back sharply. She tasted blood in her mouth, and felt several loose teeth. The soldier tossed her to the ground, and turned back to the captain and admiral.

“Last chance for this one. Give me the command codes.” The admiral refused to even look in her direction, but Captain Andrews was staring down at her and Nat could see he was about to speak. She shook her head, gaze hard as she tried to force her determination on him. She was glad to see his lips grow tight. They only needed to hold out for a minute longer, and it would be too late to reverse what she’d set in motion.

“The frigate is accelerating,” one of the soldiers on the bridge below called out. “The speed is increasing too fast, lieutenant. We’re going to shoot through the Syndicate fleet in three minutes.”

“That was brave,” the leader of the enemy soldiers said with admiration in their tone. The soldier crouched over Nat with helmet tilted as if examining her for the first time. “Brave, but foolish. All you’ve done is remove a ship from the fight and weaken your Coalition forces. The *Indomitable* is sure to wipe away all resistance now.”

She smiled up at him in defiance, feeling the blood flowing from her mouth, sure that her red-stained teeth must present a gruesome sight. It was almost a relief when the soldier drew a pistol with lighting reflexes and placed it against her temple as the trigger was pulled.

TWENTY FIVE

Erik was seated in the control center of the *Vagabond* once again, beginning to feel as if his every waking moment was spent in the command chair that part of him was starting to loathe. After a week spent on the far side of Earth hiding from the approaching Syndicate fleet, the three freighters were fully loaded and prepared for their part of the fight. President Meyers had given him command of the small group of ships, and on his orders the three set out on a curving course that saw the ships pushing their engines to the limits.

The *Cambier* was the slowest of them, limiting their advance to a four G burn that was near constant from the moment they departed the home world. Erik allowed the ships to cut to a half G burn for several hours three times each day, giving the crews a chance to move about the ships to attend to any personal needs or repairs. He had a tight deadline and refused to let the small group fall behind.

"*Montford* is signaling that they just depleted another fuel rod," Mira said during one of the low burns.

"They should have more than enough for what we're doing," Erik told her firmly. "Tell them we don't need to know about it every time they change one out."

"Sure thing, cap," she said with a light tone. He knew that ignoring his surliness was her way of making him realize how stupid he was being, and it always amazed him how well it worked.

“Thank them for the update, though. Have to keep up communication if we’re going to be effective.” Sighing and unstrapping, he stood and tried to give his body a bit of exercise. He paced back and forth in the small room, seven steps each direction before turning and going back. He was so accustomed to the normal quarter G thrust that even at half of Earth’s gravity he could feel his muscles working hard to keep him moving. A part of him started to wonder why Marines never did training simulations in heavy gravity to build stronger soldiers, but he figured there had to be a host of reasons since it had never happened.

“Both ships reporting in as ready for hard braking burn,” Mira said.

Erik returned to his chair and strapped in, pulling them tightly over the bulky compression suit he wore in an abundance of caution. “Punch it,” he called, and immediately felt the ship jump forward as the thrusters were fed power. The four G burn of the braking thrusters was enough to make him truly appreciate the work the shipyard on Luna had done. The frame of the ship was stronger than it had been since before his father rescued it from a salvage yard, cobbling together whatever repairs he could to get it into the freight lanes. He almost missed the rattles and shudders now that the ship accelerated smoothly.

He looked to a display at his side, showing that the two fleets would be meeting in around three hours. They wouldn’t know for sure until he got closer to the expected location of the battle and received the feeds that freighters scattered among the Coalition fleet sent out. That should come in an hour before the first shots, giving his small group of ships time to adjust course if necessary. He hoped it wouldn't be required, since it would lower their effectiveness.

"Tom, everything ready in the cargo bay?"

"Aye, captain," the man replied over the comm. "I'll only need a few minutes to initiate."

"I'll make sure you have them. Let's just hope our counterparts are as prepared." Erik had been over the plans ad nauseam with the other freighter captains. Each had seemed comfortable with the separate stages, but having never worked with them he was unsure of how reliable they might be. He knew they could be thinking the same of himself and his crew.

The final stages of the plan he had worked out with the president of the Guild required absolute accuracy in execution. A few seconds too soon or too late could have disastrous consequences not only for the freighters but for the rest of the Coalition fleet. It was a heavy responsibility to carry, but Erik felt more than ready for this chance to finally strike back in a way he couldn't with just the new railguns mounted on the hull of his ship.

"Communication feed coming in," Mira announced a few hours later.

"Right on time," Erik said in satisfaction as the information started to come up on the main holo display. The Syndicate fleet had held to the expected speed, but the Coalition ships had moved faster than expected in their desire for revenge after Interamnia and Mars. "Looks like we need to make adjustments, but it shouldn't be anything too major. Isaac, can you crunch the numbers and send the updated course to Mira so she can get it out to the other ships?"

"Already working on it, captain."

"Thank you." Erik was pleased to see that things were going as planned. The display showing the progress of the fleets updated and the dotted lines of projected ship locations filled in to show known locations and courses. Each ship was labeled, but the distance between the two groups was still too great for the words to be large enough to read. As the fleets grew closer, the ships would grow larger on the plotted map and make details visible.

Isaac had the updated course calculated and sent out within five minutes. Erik listened in to Mira's channel with the other pilots to make sure they acknowledged the updates and reported in that the course corrections had been made. The *Montford* was a kilometer above the *Vagabond*, with the *Cambier* the same distance below. Their formation would tighten even further as they approached the fleets until no more than a few hundred meters separated each ship. They had to make any course changes simultaneously to avoid crashing together.

Less than ten minutes from intercepting the course of the fleets, Mira called out. "The *Waterloo* just started to accelerate, cap. I can't tell what they're doing."

"Are the other Coalition ships speeding up as well?" If the fleet changed the plan of attack now, it could ruin the goal he was working toward and throw all of their tactics into disarray.

“No, they’re holding steady. The *Waterloo* is continuing to speed up, though.” Mira put the bow camera view on the main screen, and they watched as the frigate, small with the distance, continued to accelerate as it passed through the Syndicate ships. The maneuver had been such a surprise that only a few shots were fired as the frigate passed through, and the Coalition ship did not fire at all.

“Some kind of malfunction must have happened on that ship,” Erik said. “We’ll have to hope they get her under control again to help out before this is over.” He looked at the timer on several of his screens. “Coming up on the time to kill the engines. Are you ready?”

“Ready and waiting,” Mira affirmed. She had an open channel with the pilots of the other ship, and they chimed in as well that the thrusters would be cut on his mark.

“Now!” Erik cried out, and felt his body go almost weightless as the engines instantly died and the ship flipped so that she was flying backwards. The freighters were drawing closer at a painfully slow rate, timed perfectly to give them the desired spread at the critical moment while also giving them time to get the engines going again afterwards and separate.

On the display, he watched as a cloud of fighters that had been launched from the frigates minutes before crossed the dwindling space between the fleets and began to attack the Syndicate vessels. It was not a large surprise when the Syndicate ships launched their own fighters, though they had half the numbers of their opposing force.

Two minutes from his group's intercept, the fleets began to fire railgun rounds and torpedoes. The Coalition frigates were targeting the *Indomitable* while the freighters with them focused on two of the enemy frigates in an attempt to do enough damage to knock them out of the fight. On the other hand, the Syndicate ships seemed to have adopted a strategy of one at a time as they all concentrated fire on a single frigate in the other fleet.

"Tom, what's your status?"

"Ready to go, captain. Just have to push a button and all three ships will deploy."

"You're cleared to activate at the ten-second mark," Erik told him.

"Aye," Tom replied.

Erik watched the screen in impatience, the ships growing larger on the display as the rounds being fired filled the space between. Small debris fields and the occasional fiery flash showed where rounds were impacting the hulls. The Coalition frigate receiving all the attention was obviously heavily damaged already, and he could see that there appeared to be only two guns still working on that ship. The *Indomitable*, however, was holding up well under the bulk of the attack. Erik felt disheartened to see that there were at least a dozen railguns firing from the cruiser's hull, indicating that more of the guns had been brought out from Earth by the Syndicate frigates.

"Releasing now," Tom said calmly over the comms, and Erik felt a faint tremor as the cargo bay doors on the bow opened. A second later, the trio of freighters were behind the combined Coalition and freighter fleet, flying across the path that the Syndicate ships would be occupying in less than half a minute. From the open cargo bay doors of each ship, two thousand tons of loose rock and ore chunks were ejected into space. The detritus of mining operations, loads that couldn't be sold and were only used to even out the cargo pods when there was not enough valuable ores and minerals to fill them. It was perfect material to lay a deadly trap for the Syndicate fleet.

Erik knew that his small group of freighters had been seen, and that the Syndicate sensors would be blaring alarms about the cloud of rocks and ore chunks filling the path the ships were too close to deviate from. What he'd effectively created was a massive micro meteor storm that the enemy vessels were about to go through. The frigates and cruiser were moving at speeds that turned the detritus deadly, impacting the millions of small objects fast enough to create tears in the hulls of the ships.

As Mira started the thrusters again to slowly bleed off momentum so they could advance back toward the battle, Erik watched in shocked fascination as one of the Syndicate frigates was torn nearly in half as it exploded from within. The cloud of rocks and ore must have penetrated the reactor core or one of the weapon emplacements, and started a chain reaction of failure. The two other frigates he could see on this side of the massive cruiser also suffered large amounts of damage, and he could see visible holes in the hulls of both ships.

The *Indomitable* had suffered damage, but by some quirk of fate the cruiser passed through a part of the debris field that was lighter than it was elsewhere. Erik had to be satisfied at knowing he had torn the hull apart in a few dozen places, but that it would be a small hindrance for such a large ship. He could only hope some of the ship's railguns or defensive weapons had been destroyed or disabled in the random explosions he could see across the hull.

The Syndicate ships should have flipped at this point, to slow and continue firing on the Coalition fleet. It was what everyone had expected, a big battle here a week from Earth to determine which superpower would be ascendant. Instead, Erik saw the thrusters flare bright as the ships began to burn toward the home world. The line of ships was ragged now, with several of the remaining frigates seeming to struggle to reach the speed that the cruiser was pushing for.

"Shit!" he yelled. "Get us moving after them, Mira. Kick the engines as high as they'll go." The pilot grunted in acknowledgement, already working to do what he'd ordered. The *Vagabond* was slowly skewing around to follow the Syndicate fleet, but he knew from his attempted chase a few months earlier that the cruiser was faster than his freighter could ever be.

He looked back up at the main display to see the Coalition ships furiously burning to try and reverse their momentum towards the outer system. He sent out a sensor mapping of the stone and ore debris that remained after the Syndicate ships hit most of it, to ensure that the friendly ships did not collide with some of it in their haste to be after the enemy. Beacons had been scattered around within the debris, and he activated them now to provide future warning for any ships that should follow this path.

"*Montford* and *Cambier* are turning with us, cap."

"Good. Tell them to push as hard as they can to catch up, but we're not going to hold back to stay with them this time." Erik flipped the switch for the ship's comms and warned the crew to get strapped in for a maximum burn. "No breaks this time, until we catch those Syndicate ships or our engines fail."

"Cap?" Mira sounded stunned as she drew his attention again. "I have comm relays coming in from three of the freighters with the Coalition fleet.

"Make that four.

"No, five.

"All of them. I have comm relays from all of the freighters."

"Patch them all in on a single channel. Can we do that?"

"Uh, I think so." He saw her hands moving across the terminals as she worked, and he tried to think what the other freighter captains could be calling his ship for. Congratulations for the plan that they'd not known about? Asking his three ships to join the line of the fleet? Something like that would come from whoever was in charge of the frigates, though.

"Got it," Mira called triumphantly. "I pulled in the *Montford* and the *Cambier*, as well. Audio only, on now."

“This is Captain Frost of the *Vagabond*,” he said, pausing to let someone else speak. A rush of voices filled the room, some speaking normally and other almost yelling. A deep and gravelly voice finally overwhelmed the others and they all died away.

“Frost, this is Johansson on the *Viking*. You just hit the Syndicate harder than this entire fleet did in our first pass. Any more tricks like that up your sleeve?”

Erik knew the other captain by reputation only, an old veteran who was one of the first to join the Guild. “Well, we did have one other thing planned but that went out the window when the bastards decided to keep running.”

“So it’s a chase, then?”

“It is, Captain Johansson. I only hope those Coalition frigates have the speed to catch the cruiser before it reaches Earth.”

“About that,” the man paused, a hesitation that made Erik’s heart skip a beat. “The Fleet Admiral was on *Waterloo*. Our sensors show the frigate is still burning hard for the outer system, but our contact on another frigate says there have been no communications from them. No explanation for leaving the fleet at all.”

Erik sighed, and leaned his head back in his helmet. “Let me guess, the other frigate captains have no idea what to do now?”

“That’s about right from what I’ve been able to hear. Sounds like the most senior captain is over on the *Yorktown*, and she has no battle experience at all.”

"Mira, can you try and get a line open with the *Yorktown*?"

"I can try, cap." There was silence as Erik and all the freighter captains on the shared line waited in tense anticipation. The *Vagabond* was steadily increasing speed, the increased gravity slowing the process as the pilot had to switch to verbal commands with her hands now too heavy to move across the terminals. "Got her," Mira finally announced.

"This is Captain Imahara of the *Yorktown*. Who am I speaking with?"

"Ma'am, this is Captain Frost on the freighter *Vagabond*."

"*Vagabond*?" He could hear her turn away and ask faintly which of the freighters with the fleet that was. "Captain Frost, are you the one responsible for dropping all of this debris in our path?"

"If you mean in the path of the Syndicate fleet, destroying one ship and damaging most of the others, then yes."

The line was silent for a few moments. "Such an action is against the articles of war agreed upon by the nations of Earth forty years ago, captain."

"Well, ma'am, I'm not part of an Earth fleet. I'm a captain in the Transport Guild, and we're independent of all world governments. So, I say this with all respect, you can shove those articles of war and know that I'll do anything I can to stop a ship that has been very open about wanting to kill tens of thousands more people. Probably millions."

There was a mutter of agreement from the other freighter captains, alerting the frigate captain to their presence. "Why did you initiate this communication, Captain Frost?"

"Captain Imahara, you should be able to see that my ship and the two others that flew in with me are burning as hard as we can to try and catch up to the Syndicate ship. I was hoping you would tell me that you're going to be doing the same. This is one time I'll be quite happy to see a Coalition frigate speeding past my little freighter."

"We have suffered a loss of our own, Captain Frost, though it may be a temporary one. The admiral was on the ship that has inexplicably accelerated toward the outer system."

"Yes, we're all aware of the situation. You can be sure we're all equally perplexed by the *Waterloo*'s actions, Captain Imahara. But that doesn't change the fact that the Syndicate fleet has been damaged and is still burning hard for Earth."

Mira's voice sounded in his ear, on a private channel between their two comms. "The other frigates are tapping in to the line, cap. We have an audience that's quickly growing to include every ship in the combined fleet."

Imahara was sounding harassed now, and he could tell she was fighting within herself but unsure of which direction to turn. "With no communication from the Fleet Admiral, a request for orders has been sent to the prime minister's office. We'll know within an hour or two what he wishes the fleet to do in the absence of the admiral. The fleet will continue to bleed off momentum, but hold in place until those orders arrive."

Erik was angry, but also unsurprised. Never having been through a battle situation, not even the paltry fights against belt pirates, he knew the captain of the *Yorktown* lacked the experience needed for a situation like this. He doubted she could even see how fatal such an indecisive action could be.

"Captain, if you plan to just sit there with your tail tucked between your legs, then you're doing nothing but helping the Syndicate in their attempt to destroy any opposition to their domination of the system. The only thing worse than trying and failing is to not even try at all. Freighter captains, are you still on the line?" There was a chorus of ayes, along with some muttering and growling about craven actions. "The Guild agreed to work with the Coalition fleet in the defense of Earth. If the Navy is no longer working toward that end, then our contract is null and void. You're all free to join with the *Vagabond* and hope that we can make some small contribution to slow down the Syndicate."

Almost instantly, the stern cameras showed small flares of light as the freighters scattered among the Coalition frigates increased power to their engines. They could never hope to catch Erik and the two other freighters with him, but they'd know that they were doing something instead of waiting around to get orders that might never come.

"Cap," Mira yelped, struggling to raise an arm to point at the display.

"I see it," he told her, a smile spreading across his face. One of the frigates had flared its engines and was already beginning to move toward him instead of continuing to drift farther away. A second and then a third followed, and soon six of the frigates were burning at maximum power.

"Coalition captains, you will cease your actions immediately!" Captain Imahara yelled, and he knew that she had opened a channel with her cohorts, temporarily forgetting his channel was still open. "If you do not desist, these actions will constitute a mutiny and you will face court martial on return to Earth."

"All due respect, Imahara, but we don't take orders from you," one of the frigate captains said over both channels. "The last order from the Fleet Admiral was to engage the Syndicate fleet, and until I hear a counter order from another superior officer that's what I intend to do."

There was a sound of a short scuffle, and then a new voice spoke. "This is Commander Troy, on the *Yorktown*. Captain Imahara has been relieved of duty for failure to follow the orders of the Fleet Admiral. Our ship is with the fleet." Even as he spoke, all of the ships were burning hard and already beginning to accelerate toward Earth and the Syndicate fleet.

The distance was too great for him to see it, but Erik knew that the fighters not destroyed in strafing and bombing runs were returning to their ships as the fleet approached the location where they had traded shots with the Syndicate fleet. He knew it was wrong, but he felt a bit of joy to know that any Syndicate fighters that had survived the encounter would be stranded in the depths of space with engines that weren't capable of the hard acceleration needed to reach the nearest planet or moon before air and fuel supplies were exhausted. They might surrender to the frigates to save themselves, but would have to act quickly.

"Channel's closed," Mira reported.

"How does it look? Do we have any chance of intercept before that cruiser reaches Luna and Earth?"

"Assuming they travel at the same speed as when they left Interamnia, we're going to arrive twenty-seven hours after they do. The Coalition frigates, however, should be able to intercept several hours out from Earth."

"Let's hope they're able to do enough to stop the *Indomitable*, or at least slow it down so the rest of us can join the fight."

TWENTY SIX

Four days after the Coalition fleet left Earth in a mad rush toward a meeting with the advancing Syndicate ships, the protests and riots outside Aldrin's administrative building turned deadly. A group of young men had been agitating the crowd for hours, demanding answers from the administrator about the bombings at the docking facility and the transit tunnel. The continued silence from within the building may have been calculated to cool tempers, but instead it was doing the reverse and causing more frustration and anger. The sight of silent Marines holding weapons with twitchy fingers only millimeters from the triggers did not help matters, either.

President Meyers had continued bringing in shipments of supplies and people from the planet below. By the end of the first week, more than a hundred proved brave enough and signed up to join the Transport Guild and get shipped to Luna. Most were put to work helping with repairs on the docking facility and landing pads, now under Guild control. Two small squads had been formed and armed to provide protection around the Guildhall and the repair work. The nightly sabotages that set back the rebuilding had stopped as soon as there were armed patrols keeping an eye on the area, which was only more frustrating since it could have been done weeks earlier if the Coalition Marines had bothered to spare one soldier each shift.

Dex was officially promoted to second in command of the Guild, working closely with Meyers every day. She coordinated the five freighters that continued meeting small cargo shuttles from the blue and green surface of the planet below. It took several hours for each freighter to land on the rough surface of Luna, get everyone suited up in EVA gear, and then march across the surface to the temporary airlock and decontamination hub. Fine lunar dust had to be swept clear of the pressure suits and cargo containers, ejected back out into the lunar atmosphere. The sharp edges of particles that had never suffered air or water erosion could prove deadly if they filled the air of the dome and were breathed in to fragile human lungs.

On the fifth day after the frigates departed, the docking facility repairs reached a point where one small landing pad had been set up and could connect to the dome with a new docking collar and tube. The rigid apparatus that they'd been able to procure was not as versatile as the flexible docking tubes in use across the system, but still allowed for much faster ingress and egress than the temporary airlock hub. Now, Dex could have freighters land and unload in under an hour.

They still had the crate full of flechette rifles the *Vagabond* had been carrying for the cruiser, but the lethal weapons were viewed as a last resort. Procuring stun weapons for the Guild's new militia arm had been challenging, but not as difficult as finding body armor. The suppliers of the specialized gear had exclusive contracts with the Navy and Marines of the two superpowers, and would not even take her calls to consider offers to supply the Transport Guild. People thought of the Guild as no more than space truckers, and could see no reason they should need to meet with arms and armor manufacturers.

Her only resort was buying what she could from the black market on Earth, dealing with intermediaries who had their own intermediaries. It used up more than half the budget Meyers had set aside for the militia, but she'd managed to cobble together six full suits of used armor and a few dozen stun pistols.

When the violence across the square started that evening, no one thought it more than a brief release of the pressure that had been building up. A bottle was thrown from within the crowd, heavy bio plastic filled with liquid to give it more mass, and smashed against the visor of one of the Marines. The man yelped in surprise, holding up a hand to wipe at blood that was streaming from a nose smashed under the sturdy face plate.

If he'd merely gone into the administrative building for first aid, things might have ended there and returned to a yelling crowd confronting silent Marines. Instead, the same frustration and anger fueling the crowd had been building up in Marines who hated being pulled away from finding out who had killed their friends in the bombing. There had been no outlet available, and so the attack of the thrown bottle caused the Marine to scream out his frustration. He raised his flechette rifle and fired blindly into the crowd.

His partner several yards away thought he was firing to fend off an attack, and turned her own rifle on the crowd. In that moment, she saw the expressions of fear and surprise as anger and hatred. The crowd pushed toward her as people tried to flee from the square. She thought people were rushing to attack her, and began to fire her own flechette rounds into the unarmed crowd of civilians.

Screams of pain and fear drew Dex to the doorway of the Guildhall, a building she rarely left these days. All she could see from her vantage point was that the crowd was agitated and moving around more than usual. "What happened?" she asked one of the militia guards flanking the door.

"I think I heard shots," the man said, craning his head to try and see over the crowd. "Maybe, but it was so quiet and so fast it could have been anything."

"Probably some damn fool using the noise to try inciting the crowds, and it looks like it's working." Dex frowned as she watched the swirling mass of people. It seemed as if most were trying to push backward to get away from the crush, and she saw people sprint from the square in ones and twos. Those at the rear of the crowds were only trying to push forward, though, just as unaware of what was going on as she was. Half the dome's population seemed to be clustered in the small square.

Another militia guard stepped forward and spoke in disbelief. "Report from the roof, ma'am. The Marines are firing into the crowd. With lethal rounds."

"What?!" Dex snapped her head around to look at him, and could see her shock mirrored in his expression. "Get another person on the roof to keep reporting, and call in the rest of the militia. Three on duty at the docks, and everyone else here in case this escalates."

Turning, she ran back into the Guildhall and rushed through the long room to barge into the president's office. Meyers was spread out on his couch, a thin blanket pulled over him as he dozed and tried to get what little rest he could. Her loud entry made him sit up, staring at her with startled eyes. "What's going on, Dex?"

"The Marines are firing into the crowd of protesters, sir. Our guard on the roof says lethal rounds, but I don't know any more."

"Son of a bitch!" Meyers yelled, throwing the blanket aside and jumping up to run from the room. He led the way to a narrow stairway that led to the roof, twenty feet above the square. As they exited, the nearest militia guard whirled to point her stun pistol at them. She lowered the weapon at the sight the Guild leader, and turned back to look out over the square.

Dex approached the short wall that lined the top of the building, and was flabbergasted to find at least a dozen people lying on the ground in front of the barrier. The panic had spread through the crowd, and the push backwards was finally gaining momentum, more and more people pushing to leave the square. The full squad of Marines was now standing behind the barrier, weapons raised and pointed at the fleeing crowd, though they weren't firing any longer. From the blood pooling on the ground, Dex had no doubt the protesters left behind were either dead or quickly dying.

"Why don't they send out a medic?" she asked in a half whisper.

"Heat of the moment, ma'am," the militia guard answered. "The adrenaline has them so keyed up all they can think about is their own squad, and they only see enemies before them." The woman shrugged as she spoke. "I spent a year as a Marine guard on a base, and it's an attitude you develop quickly without even realizing it."

"What started it?" Meyers asked roughly.

"I think I saw one of the protesters throw something, and it hit one of the Marines. It was like the man just went mad, and he started firing at the crowd. The other Marine followed suit maybe fifteen seconds later. The rest of the squad started to run out of the building then. None of them fired but they didn't really try to stop it, either. I think it's their sergeant who finally called for a ceasefire."

"This is exactly what I feared would happen," Meyers said through tightly clenched teeth. "Everyone's losing their grip, and things are going to descend into total anarchy if someone doesn't step forward and take control. I'd hoped the administration or the Marines would come to their senses, but it looks like it will have to be the Guild instead." He turned as another militia guard exited the stairwell onto the roof. "Keep a watch on the Marines tonight, and let me know if they make any movements to leave their barricaded area."

Dex followed her president down the stairs and into his office. Meyers plopped down on the couch and rubbed his hands over his face, while she poured a shot of whiskey for them both. "Thanks," he said, taking the offered glass.

"We aren't set up to be a military group," Dex said quietly. "We have twelve guards armed with stun pistols and batons, only six of them with low-quality armor. That squad of Marines could shred our militia easily."

"I know. This isn't the kind of thing I was planning for, Dex. I just wanted some kind of show of force to keep the Guildhall safe in case the riots turned into looting, and to keep the docking facility repairs protected from whoever was sabotaging the efforts there. We get paid to ship things from one place to another, not police a dome of more than two thousand people. But I also can't sit by and let the Coalition Marines kill citizens just because someone threw a bottle."

Dex felt the burn of the liquor in her throat, rolling the empty glass between her hands. "If we pull in the people we have working on the docks, I could pass out a dozen more stun pistols. At least our militia would look more intimidating then."

"It's something to keep in mind. Let's hope cooler heads prevail and the administrator holds the Marines accountable for their actions. Whatever statement they release tomorrow is going to tell us if they plan to follow the laws or try to enact some kind of martial law in the dome." Meyers drained his glass and slammed it on the corner of his desk. "I just wish we knew what was going on over in Armstrong. No information at all is coming through?"

"Nothing is getting to the *Guild*," Dex clarified. "I don't know if the dome administrator's office is able to contact their counterpart, or if they're getting news relayed through Earth."

"Okay, then we work with what we have. Our representative in the prime minister's office is being shut out of meetings now, and it looks like both sides have decided that the Guild has no purpose or use in their conflict. If that's how they want to treat us, then I'm quite happy to take matters into my own hands. I think it might be time for us to take the Guild to the next level."

"Do you mean form our own faction?" Dex asked in resignation, having seen the signs of this moment approaching for weeks.

"The way I see it, we only have two options. Carry on as we are now, and continue to be beaten down into irrelevance until we have no choice but disband the Guild. Or become something more than a simple collection of freighters working for the highest bidder, and establish our place in the system completely outside the Coalition and Syndicate dynamic."

"There's going to be backlash from some of the captains," she cautioned. "They're in it for the money they make from hauling cargo, not for the political aspects."

"I'm ready for that when it happens, but I think most of our crews are aware enough of what's going on in the system this last year to know that sitting on the sidelines isn't a viable option any longer. We already committed most of our fleet to working with the Coalition frigates to stop that Syndicate cruiser. This is just the next step, where we declare that we will continue to remain independent."

"This is going to be a large undertaking, sir. An expensive one, as well."

"Indeed, that it will. I'm putting you in charge of organizing things, Dex. We'll discuss budgets and all of that after whatever announcement comes out of the administrator's office tomorrow."

The next day brought no statements at all, as the dome administration continued their policy of total silence. The Marine guards were still in place, blood staining the ground where bodies had been dragged away in the small hours when the local medical staff were finally called out to dispose of them. Dex took time away from her duties to visit the medical clinic and view the bodies of the protestors.

"They weren't all dead," the orderly escorting her blurted out.

"What?"

"They didn't all die when they were shot." He couldn't meet her eyes as he spoke. "When we arrived to pick up the bodies, it was obvious that some of the people had crawled from where they fell, trying to get away. Three of them were still alive when the crowd dispersed, and probably lived for half an hour or more with their wounds."

Dex felt her teeth grinding together with rage. "You're saying that if the Marines had bothered to perform basic first aid, three of these people could still be alive?"

"At least three, maybe more." The orderly turned away, as if refusing to look at the bodies laid out on the racks of the medical center's morgue.

She stormed back to the Guildhall with growing anger and frustration, and stomped into Meyers' office to find him on a video call with one of his many contacts on the planet below. He took one look at her face and hastily ended the call, to listen in growing horror as she told him what she'd learned.

"That's it," he said with finality. "The people of this dome deserve better than to be gunned down just because some hooligan throws a bottle that happens to hit a Marine. The fact that the administrator's office is saying nothing tells me that they don't care about the people killed. They only want to keep a tight hold on their control of the dome."

He crossed the office and opened a cabinet that had been locked, needing two keys to access it. Pulling out a thick package, he tossed it at Dex. "That's the plan I've been working up for years. I'd hoped to never have to put it into action, but the choice has been made for us. I put it all on paper to ensure that there was no trace of it in our computer systems."

Dex hefted the package, thick enough that it had to contain several hundred sheets of paper. She knew it would take her weeks to read through and wrap her head around everything there.

"This is your only priority for the time being," Meyers said. "Get someone to start coordinating the freighters and take over all the other jobs I know you've been overloading yourself with. If there are still people refusing to leave their homes after the bombings, try and get them work that they can do via a remote connection. I'm sure that by now most of them are hurting for credits with prices going up on goods all over Aldrin."

“There is one other thing I’d like to keep working on,” she told him. “That project I’ve been coordinating for Erik, the research from his friend that was killed on Interamnia.”

“Ah, I forgot all about that. Making progress with it?”

Dex smiled, the grin spreading slowly. “Big progress. They built a small scale prototype a while back, and it’s been working like a charm. Next stage is a full-scale reactor, which is already in progress.”

“Excellent! Keep me in the loop on that when you hear about their progress.”

Feeling resolute, she left the office to start passing off most of the jobs she had been handling for the Guild. Afterward, she left to return to her small apartment for the first time in a week, a place where she could read through the thick documents without distraction and start working on plans to put the proposals into effective practice.

Two days later, the news of the first engagement between the fleets arrived. Erik sent her a message talking about how well the debris field had worked against the Syndicate ships, joy suffusing his face and making her smile in reply as she watched him speak on the screen. The news that the Syndicate fleet had continued burning for Earth and the delay in the Coalition fleet moving to catch them was disheartening. She saw it on the faces of others she passed within Aldrin when the news trickled down to the citizens of the dome. The people had thought they were safe when the fleet left orbit around Earth and Luna, but instead they were still facing the same danger with no defenses at all now.

Freighters dropping off supplies were suddenly bringing in fewer new people to join the Guild. Instead, they were getting paid to take people away from Luna as citizens began to flee for the safety of the home world below. With the Syndicate cruiser still advancing, few held out hope that their home could be saved.

Twenty Seven

Erik couldn't believe what he was seeing on the main holo displays. The *Indomitable* had held back so the hobbled Syndicate frigates could stay in formation for days, but now the cruiser was feeding more power into her thrusters and breaking off to move ahead of the fleet. He watched in dismay as the tracking and projection countdown for when it approached Earth began to shrink in large chunks. "They're going to reach Earth before the Coalition frigates can catch up," he said.

"Yeah, cap. I'm betting they saw the fleet catching up and decided to let their remaining frigates slow down the Coalition ships."

"Is there any sign of the Coalition fleet slowing?"

Mira was silent as she looked through her data, limited to voice and eye movement commands with the *Vagabond* burning at almost eight G's as they tried to catch the cruiser. "Uh, it looks like they're actually speeding up? I didn't think they had anything more in the tanks, but a few of the frigates are pulling ahead of the others now."

"Good, maybe they can limit the damage the *Indomitable* is able to do. They can get off some shots as they pass those Syndicate frigates, wound them even more."

That clash was fast approaching now, and he could only wish the Guild freighters had ion engines powerful enough to keep up with the military vessels. The *Vagabond* was far in front of the strung out freighters, but still over seven hours behind the Coalition frigates at this point of the chase. He could only watch the sensor data and fuzzy images from the zoomed in bow camera as the frigates approached each other.

"The Syndicate ships are slowing!" Mira said in surprise. "It looks like they're flipping to face the Coalition ships as they pass."

Tiny flashes flared all across the display, railguns and torpedoes firing into each fleet from their opposite number. Erik knew his trap with the field of rocks and ore chunks had left the Syndicate frigates damaged, though he couldn't be sure of the severity. It proved to have been greater than he'd hoped, as he saw first one and then a second frigate break apart under the rain of projectiles from the swiftly approaching Coalition fleet.

What he hadn't anticipated was that the expanding field of debris from the destroyed vessels created an obstacle that was too near for the Coalition frigates to avoid. Several of them passed through the debris fields and suffered more damage within half a minute than they might have in half an hour of hard fighting. He saw the ion thrusters fade away on the port engines of one frigate, sending it veering off to starboard where it collided with another ship. At the intense speeds the vessels were traveling, any collision was fatal. This one was spectacularly so, the front of one frigate shearing off thousands of chunks of metal and plastics while the other crumpled and then exploded in a bright flash of light as the nuclear reactor core exploded.

"Damn it!" Erik yelled out, feeling his body tensely attempting to lean forward against the heavy gravity, as if trying to urge his ship to move faster and join the fight.

Depleted uranium and tungsten alloy railgun rounds continued to be fired from the surviving frigates. The Syndicate captains seemed resigned to losing their ships, and abandoned all caution to attack with ferocity. Two Coalition frigates made it past with minor damage, still firing from rear-facing guns as they continued to rush after the *Indomitable*.

A third frigate was passing above the fray, seemingly out of danger, when a Syndicate frigate fired ventral bow thrusters to throw the front of the ship into the path of the Coalition frigate. The ships scraped together, a line of debris spreading out from where the bow of the Syndicate ship plowed a furrow through the belly of its enemy, all the while continuing to fire railgun rounds into the wounded ship. The Coalition vessel made it through the battlefield, but from the way it failed to correct a course altered by the collision, Erik could tell that there would be massive casualties aboard and it would not be a part of the further fight against the cruiser.

Another Syndicate frigate slowed their rate of fire as Coalition rounds damaged their gun emplacements or decimated the crew in the damaging strikes, leaving only one to face the last two Coalition frigates that would be zipping past in no more than a minute. Erik cheered them on silently, hoping they would only damage this last enemy and leave it for the freighters to take down when they finally arrived like scavengers on a battlefield.

He flinched when the Syndicate ship exploded violently, fate or planning bringing the explosion at the very moment the Coalition ships were perfectly placed to receive the bulk of the debris in their paths. Erik had to turn his head as he saw one of the frigates break apart into at least a dozen pieces. The other seemed to continue on, but he knew there would be grievous wounds across the hull of the ship.

"My God," Mira breathed out. "Only three Coalition ships left after all that, and one of them probably not worth much after passing through that explosion. Is it going to be enough?"

Erik sighed and shook his head as much as possible inside his helmet. He had been entertaining the same dire thoughts. "It all depends on how many guns the Syndicate was able to send out with the fleet from Earth and get mounted on the *Indomitable*. If that cruiser is even half armed, it will be evenly matched with what's left of the Coalition fleet."

"I hope the frigates have the advantage, for the sake of everyone in Aldrin dome on Luna. That has to be their next target."

"Maybe. I think the Syndicate admiral might have to change his plans at this point, with the wolves following behind and the door only open for perhaps one strike against the Coalition."

"You think he'll go right to hitting the major cities?"

"I would, if I were an evil bastard." Erik twisted his lips, feeling dirty even thinking about it. He knew that with more than half their fleet destroyed or disabled, the Coalition government would be feeling apprehensive about the damage the Syndicate cruiser could do. It might take only one strong example to make them fold under the pressure, and then all this effort and loss in attempts to stop the Syndicate advance would have been for nothing.

The *Montfort* signaled that they would stop to check on the disabled Coalition frigate, while the *Cambier* would remain with his ship as they raced to Earth to try and assist the remaining Coalition fleet. He sent a message back to the captain of the *Montfort* to remind him to be wary of the remaining Syndicate frigates. If they got just one railgun repaired and workable, they could cause large amounts of damage to the Guild ships that approached. Six of the freighters began to slow, preparing to stop and ensure the Syndicate frigates were truly out of the fight. Together, they could all match a fully functional frigate, and two greatly damaged vessels should be no threat to their combined firepower.

When the *Vagabond* passed by the steadily expanding debris field from the battle, the entire crew was watching on monitors throughout the ship as they got a close up view of the devastation. Nine frigates destroyed or disabled, more than half of both Earth fleets taken out in a single fifteen-minute battle. Thousands were dead, thousands more possibly wounded, and all of it because one government decided that the other had to be removed no matter how many lives would be lost in the process.

"Things can't go on like this," Erik said quietly to himself. Whatever the outcome of the days to come, he knew that things in the system would be changing in a dramatic fashion. Even if the Syndicate could be stopped, faith and trust in the government of the Coalition was also eroded and he didn't know if they could survive or would also be toppled to be replaced by something new. Perhaps Earth would return to the hundreds of fragmented countries it had been a century before, fighting amongst themselves over resources and beliefs while the people of the colonies and planets beyond governed themselves.

The *Vagabond* hurtled on, eagerly approaching Earth with a hope to be in at the end.

ACKNOWLEDGEMENTS

I would like to once again thank Bethany Wright for her awesome editing. She took my rough second draft and gave me a lot of suggestions and options of ways to improve the story.

I'd also like to thank Christopher Doll for the awesome cover art on this series. I highly recommend checking his site for some great stuff. I get lost in there for long stretches, looking at the fantastic art.

www.christopher-doll.com

About The Author

Tim has been a dreamer since he was a small boy, and is finally putting all his wild imaginings onto paper. During the day, he is an IT support technician for a nationwide bank. At night, he bangs away on his keyboard and often obsesses over the proper word to express an idea or feeling.

He can be found online at www.timrangnow.com, where you can sign up for a newsletter to keep up with the latest news and exclusive extras.

Guild Series

Vagabond

Indomitable

Waterloo

Resolute

Made in the USA
Coppell, TX
05 March 2023

13813144R00155